高一同學的目標

1. 熟背「高中常用7000字」

2. 月期考得高分

3. 會說流利的英語

1.「用會話背7000字①」書+ CD 280元

以三個極短句為一組的方式，讓同學背了會話，同時快速增加單字。高一同學要從「國中常用2000字」挑戰「高中常用7000字」，加強單字是第一目標。

2.「一分鐘背9個單字」書+ CD 280元

利用字首、字尾的排列，讓你快速增加單字。一次背9個比背1個字簡單。

3. rival

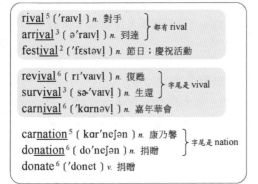

rival⁵〔ˈraɪvḷ〕n. 對手
arrival³〔əˈraɪvḷ〕n. 到達　　都有 rival
festival²〔ˈfɛstəvḷ〕n. 節日；慶祝活動

revival⁶〔rɪˈvaɪvḷ〕n. 復甦
survival³〔səˈvaɪvḷ〕n. 生還　　字尾是 vival
carnival⁶〔ˈkɑrnəvḷ〕n. 嘉年華會

carnation⁵〔kɑrˈneʃən〕n. 康乃馨
donation⁶〔doˈneʃən〕n. 捐贈　　字尾是 nation
donate⁶〔ˈdonet〕v. 捐贈

3.「一口氣考試英語」書+ CD 280元

把大學入學考試題目編成會話，背了以後，會說英語，又會考試。

例如：

What a nice surprise!（真令人驚喜！）【常考】
I can't believe my eyes.
（我無法相信我的眼睛。）
Little did I dream of seeing you here.
（做夢也沒想到會在這裡看到你。）【駒澤大】

4.「一口氣背文法」書＋CD 280元

英文文法範圍無限大，規則無限多，誰背得完？劉毅老師把文法整體的概念，編成216句，背完了會做文法題、會說英語，也會寫作文。既是一本文法書，也是一本會話書。

1. 現在簡單式的用法

I *get up* early every day.
我每天早起。

I *understand* this rule now.
我現在了解這條規定了。

Actions *speak* louder than words.
行動勝於言辭。

【二、三句強調實踐早起】

5.「高中英語聽力測驗①」書＋MP3 280元

6.「高中英語聽力測驗進階」書＋MP3 280元

高一月期考聽力佔20%，我們根據大考中心公布的聽力題型編輯而成。

7.「高一月期考英文試題」書 280元

收集建中、北一女、師大附中、中山、成功、景美女中等各校試題，並聘請各校名師編寫模擬試題。

8.「高一英文克漏字測驗」書 180元

9.「高一英文閱讀測驗」書 180元

全部取材自高一月期考試題，英雄所見略同，重複出現的機率很高。附有翻譯及詳解，不必查字典，對錯答案都有明確交待，做完題目，一看就懂。

高二同學的目標──提早準備考大學

1. 「用會話背7000字①②」
   書+CD，每冊280元

   「用會話背7000字」能夠解決
   所有學英文的困難。高二同學
   可先從第一冊開始背，第一冊
   和第二冊沒有程度上的差異，
   背得越多，單字量越多，在腦

海中的短句越多。每一個極短句大多不超過5個字，1個字或
2個字都可以成一個句子，如：「用會話背7000字①」p.184，
每一句都2個字，好背得不得了，而且與生活息息相關，是
每個人都必須知道的知識，例如：成功的秘訣是什麼？

11. What are the keys to success?

Be *ambitious*.	要有**雄心**。
Be *confident*.	要有**信心**。
Have *determination*.	要有**決心**。
Be *patient*.	要有**耐心**。
Be *persistent*.	要有**恆心**。
Show *sincerity*.	要有**誠心**。
Be *charitable*.	要有**愛心**。
Be *modest*.	要**虛心**。
Have *devotion*.	要**專心**。

當你背單字的時候，就要有「雄心」，要「決心」背好，對
自己要有「信心」，一定要有「耐心」和「恆心」，背書時
要「專心」。

背完後，腦中有2,160個句子，那不得了，無限多的排列組
合，可以寫作文。有了單字，翻譯、閱讀測驗、克漏字都難
不倒你了。高二的時候，要下定決心，把7000字背熟、背
爛。雖然高中課本以7000字為範圍，編書者為了便宜行事，
往往超出7000字，同學背了少用的單字，反倒忽略真正重要
的單字。千萬記住，背就要背「高中常用7000字」，背完之
後，天不怕、地不怕，任何考試都難不倒你。

2.「時速破百單字快速記憶」書 250元

字尾是 try，重音在倒數第三音節上

entry [3] ('ɛntrɪ) *n.* 進入【No entry. 禁止進入。】
country [1] ('kʌntrɪ) *n.* 國家；鄉下【ou 讀 /ʌ/，為例外字】
ministry [4] ('mɪnɪstrɪ) *n.* 部【mini = small】

chemistry [4] ('kɛmɪstrɪ) *n.* 化學
geometry [5] (dʒɪ'amətrɪ) *n.* 幾何學【geo 土地，metry 測量】
industry [2] ('ɪndəstrɪ) *n.* 工業；勤勉【這個字重音常唸錯】

poetry [1] ('po‧ɪtrɪ) *n.* 詩
poultry [4] ('poltrɪ) *n.* 家禽 ⎬ 字尾 y 表「集合名詞」
pastry [5] ('pestrɪ) *n.* 糕餅

3.「高二英文克漏字測驗」書 180元

4.「高二英文閱讀測驗」書 180元
全部選自各校高二月期考試題精華，英雄所見略同，再出現的機率很高。

5.「7000字學測試題詳解」書 250元
一般模考題為了便宜行事，往往超出7000字範圍，無論做多少份試題，仍然有大量生字，無法進步。唯有鎖定7000字為範圍的試題，才會對準備考試有幫助。每份試題都經「劉毅英文」同學實際考過，效果奇佳。附有詳細解答，單字標明級數，對錯答案都有明確交待，不需要再查字典，做完題目，再看詳解，快樂無比。

6.「高中常用7000字解析【豪華版】」書 390元
按照「大考中心高中英文參考詞彙表」編輯而成。難背的單字有「記憶技巧」、「同義字」及「反義字」，關鍵的單字有「典型考題」。大學入學考試核心單字，以紅色標記。

7.「高中7000字測驗題庫」書 180元
取材自大規模考試，解答詳盡，節省查字典的時間。

修 編 序

近年來「大學入學學科能力測驗」及「指定科目考試」增加了「翻譯題」，過去由於怕批改不公平，因為一句中文往往有無限多的英文翻譯，所以不考翻譯題，很高興大考中心能夠突破困難。根據以往的經驗，大考中心每研發出一種新題型，都會維持好幾年。現在高中學生，一定要開始加強翻譯訓練，否則就會吃虧。

翻譯是在語言學習中，很重要的一環。要學會翻譯，就要不斷地練習。本書將複雜的英文文法，濃縮成 800 個句子。我們按照文法規則分類，讀者利用練習翻譯的機會，也熟練了文法，而且背了這些句子，對英文作文也有幫助，一石多鳥。

本書經過特別編排，讀者第一遍可以看著中文，唸出英文；第二遍看著中文，默寫英文。也可以在每一回中抽一句，來自己練習。書中 p.161 後，從 Test 1 至 Test 77，我們收集了所有考過的題目，包含英翻中和中翻英。只要熟讀本書，勤做練習題，什麼翻譯題都難不倒你。編者建議你看英文唸的時候，要大聲讀出聲音來，再看中文，大聲朗讀英文，這樣子進步很快，你不妨試一試。

本書雖經審慎校閱，疏漏之處，恐在所難免，誠盼各界先進不吝指正。

修編者　謹識

目　錄

1. Tense

（1）——————————————————————————————— 現在式

1. I usually **have** bacon and eggs, a slice of bread, and a cup of coffee for breakfast.

2. The teacher **told** us that the earth **is** round and that it **moves** around the sun.

3. I **don't** know if he **will** carry out the plan, but if he does I'll help him by all means.

4. We **spend** three days in Chicago and **leave** for Seattle.

5. Tom **resembles** his father.

6. All work and no play **makes** Jack a dull boy.

（2）——————————————————————————————— 過去式

7. Mary **sat up** late last night, so she **got up** later than usual this morning.

8. I **finished** reading the book just now.

9. "When **did** you buy the book?" "I **bought** it the day before yesterday."

10. The teacher **told** us that the Civil War **broke out** in 1861.

【註】1.～6.用現在式的場合 1.現在的習慣。 2.表不變的眞理，與主要子句的時式無關。 3.表「時間或條件」的副詞子句，其未來動作用現在式表示。 *carry out* "實行" *by all means* "一定" 4.表極可能不變的未來。 5.＝Tom *takes after* his father. resemble 不可用在進行式中，因是

1. 時　式

（1）────────────────────────────── 現在式

1. 我早餐通常吃培根加蛋，一片麵包和一杯咖啡。

2. 老師告訴我們，地球是圓的，並且繞著太陽運轉。

3. 我不知道他是否會實行那計畫，不過如果他做了，我一定會幫助他。

4. 我們在芝加哥三天，然後到西雅圖去。

5. 湯姆像他父親。

6. 只工作而不遊戲，會使人變得遲鈍。〔諺〕

（2）────────────────────────────── 過去式

7. 瑪麗昨晚很晚才睡，所以今天早上比平常晚起。

8. 我剛剛看完這本書。

9. 「你什麼時候買這本書的？」「前天買的。」

10. 老師告訴我們，南北戰爭在 1861 年爆發。

及物動詞，所以不須介系詞。　7. ～ 10. 用過去式的場合　7. *sit up late* "很晚睡覺"　8. *just now* "剛剛" 動詞用過去式。　10. 表歷史上的事實，時式和事情發生的時間一致。　*break out* "（戰爭的）爆發"

(3) ———————————————————————————————————— 現在完成式

11. Five years *have passed* since I came to Taipei.

12. We *have* never *heard* Dick speak ill of others.

13. I *have told* you several times that you must give up smoking, haven't I ?

14. Man *has come* to know a variety of things except himself.

15. It *has been raining* hard since last night.

(4) ———————————————————————————————————— 過去完成式

16. My friends were kind enough to help me, so I got through the job sooner than I *had expected*.

17. The bicycle he bought yesterday was more expensive than the one I *had bought* the day before.

(5) ———————————————————————————————————— 進行式

18. It *is getting* dark. We must find somewhere to put up for the night.

19. They *will have been working* on the project for a year next Friday.

20. I *am leaving* for New York this evening. I *will be giving* a concert at this time tomorrow.

〔註〕11. ～ 15. 現在完成式 (have + p.p.) 表示過去繼續到現在的經驗、動作或狀態，或現在剛剛完成的動作。 11. = It is five years since I came to Taipei. 12. *speak ill of* 「說某人的壞話」 13. *give up* + *V-ing* 「放棄～；戒～」 16. 17. 過去完成式 (had + p.p.) 表示過去一定時間以前的動作或狀態。 16. *get through* "完成" 18. 現在進行式表現在繼續中的

(3) ——————————————————————————————— 現在完成式

11. 自從我來台北，已經過五年了。

12. 我們從來沒聽過狄克說別人的壞話。

13. 我已經告訴你好幾次你一定要戒煙，有沒有？

14. 人類除了自己以外，已經知道了各種不同的事。

15. 從昨晚開始，雨一直下得很大。

(4) ——————————————————————————————— 過去完成式

16. 我的朋友都很好意幫助我,因此我比我預料中要快地完成那工作。

17. 他昨天買的那輛脚踏車，比我前一天買的那輛要貴。

(5) ——————————————————————————————— 進行式

18. 天漸漸暗了。我們必須找個地方過夜。

19. 到了下星期五，他們從事那項計畫將滿一年。

20. 今天晚上我要前往紐約。明天的這個時候將舉行一場音樂會。

動作。*put up*"住宿"　19. 爲未來完成進行式（will have been + V-ing），敍述某動作將繼續到未來某時，並暗示該動作在未來某時，可能還在繼續進行。
20. *give a concert*"舉行音樂會"

2. Voice

（1）———————————————————————————— 被動語態

21. Most of the buildings in the town were **destroyed** by the fires in 1940.

22. A new school building **is** now **being built** and it **will have been finished** by next April.

23. The welcome party **will be held** at the city hall at 6 o'clock this evening.

24. Dick **has never been heard** to speak ill of others.

25. By the time we arrived, all the work **had been completed**.

（2）———————————————————————————— 不可用錯的被動語態

26. I **was caught in a shower** on my way home and **was drenched to the skin**.

27. Four persons **were killed** and more than ten persons **were** severely **injured** in the accident.

28. Mary **was** greatly **disappointed at** the result.

29. Washington, D.C. **is situated on** the Potomac River.

30. When you **are tired of** the busy life in the city, go down to the shore for a week or so.

【註】　22. 進行式的被動語態為「be being ＋ p.p.」，未來完成式的被動語態「will have been ＋ p.p.」表動作未來將完成。24. 現在完成式的被動語態「have been ＋ p.p.」，此句為第 12 句的被動語態，注意 speak 前要加 to。 25. 過去完成式的被動語態「had been ＋ p.p.」。 26. ～ 30. 有些動詞以被動語態表示主動意義，其後通常接 at, of, in 等。如：**be surprised at** "感驚訝",

2. 語　　態

（1）——————————————————————————— 被動語態

21. 城裏大部分的建築物都毀於 1940 年的火災。

22. 一棟新的學校建築正在建造當中，它將在明年四月完工。

23. 歡迎會將於今晚六點，在市政廳舉行。

24. 狄克從沒被聽說過講別人的壞話。（沒聽說過狄克講別人的壞話。）
25. 在我們到達之前，所有的工作都完成了。

（2）——————————————————————————— 不可用錯的被動語態

26. 我在回家的路上遇到驟雨，渾身都濕透了。

27. 那場意外中，有四人死亡，十多個人重傷。

28. 瑪麗對那結果大感失望。
29. 華盛頓位於波多馬克河畔。
30. 當你厭倦了都市的繁忙生活，到海邊去住一個星期左右。

---

be interested in "對～感興趣"　26. *be caught in a shower* "為驟雨所困" *on one's way home* "某人回家途中"　*be drenched to the skin* "渾身濕透"　28. *be disappointed at* "對～感到失望"　29. *be situated on* "座落於"　30. *be tired of* "厭倦" cf. *be tired with* ～ "因～而疲倦"

(3)——————————————————————————— 應注意的被動語態

31. The president *is well spoken of* and *is looked up to*
    by all the members.

32. Frank *is looked upon* as our leader and so his opinion
    is always *made much of*.

33. *It is said* that traveling by plane is about six times
    as safe as traveling by car.

34 Traveling by plane *is said* to be about six times as
    safe as traveling by car.

35. I never dreamed of Mr. White *being elected* President
    of the country.

36. *Let* it *be done* at once.

37. Tom *had* his house *broken into* last night.

38. I *have* my car *washed* every Sunday.

(4)——————————————————————————— 表被動的主動語態

39. This book *sells* well.

40. This cloth *washes* well.

───

〔註〕31. 32. 為動詞群的被動語態，31. *speak well of*～ " 說～的好話 " 的被動語
態為 be well spoken of。 *look up to* = respect " 尊敬 " *make much of*
" 尊重 " 33. 34. 為 People（They）say ～的被動語態。例如：They say
that he lives in Hawaii. → It is said that he lives in Hawaii. or
He is said to live in Hawaii. 36. 命令句的被動語態「 Let ～be ＋

（3）――――――――――――――――――――――― 應注意的被動語態

31. 那會長頗受全體會員的好評和尊敬。

32. 法蘭克被視爲我們的領袖，因此他的意見總是很受重視。

33. 據說搭飛機旅行是坐車旅行的六倍安全。

34. 據說搭飛機旅行是坐車旅行的六倍安全。

35. 我做夢也沒想到懷特先生會當選爲這個國家的總統。

36. 立刻做那事。

37. 湯姆家昨晚有人闖入。

38. 每星期日我都叫人洗我的車子。

（4）――――――――――――――――――――――― 表被動的主動語態

39. 這本書銷路很好。

40. 這塊布很好洗。

---

p.p.」。cf. 主動語態爲 Do it at once.　37. 38.「have ＋物＋ p.p.」
"使（物）被～"（表示自己不做而他人做）　37. *break into* "闖入"
39. 40. 爲表被動的主動語態，有些不及物動詞含有被動意味。　39. *sell
well* "銷路好"　40. *wash well* "好洗"

3. Auxiliary

（1）————————————————————————— will 和 shall

41. *Shall I* take care of your dog while you are away ?
42. If you like it, you *shall* have it.
43. *Will you* do me a favor ?
44. If you don't have a pen, a pencil *will do*.

（2）————————————————————————— would 和 should

45. Do as you *would* be done by.
46. Dan *would* sit for hours, silent and absent-minded, taking no notice of anyone.
47. I *would rather* die than live in dishonor.
48. The door *would not* open, however hard we tried.
49. You *should* not complain of the teacher being unhelpful. You are old enough to do it yourself.
50. The concert was a great success. You *should have come* with us.

〔註〕 41. Shall I～？ " 要我～嗎？ " 表徵求對方的意見。 *take care of* " 照顧 "
42. You shall ～，He shall ～，均表說話者的意志。You shall have it. ＝
I will give it to you. 43. Will you～？ " 你能～嗎？ " 表聽話者的意志。
44. *will do* " 可以 " 45. would ～＝wish to ～ *do by* " 對待 "
46. would 表過去的習慣。 absent-minded " 心不在焉 " *take notice of*

3. 助　動　詞

(1) ─────────────────────────────────────── will 和 shall

41. 當你不在時，要我照顧你的狗嗎？
42. 如果你喜歡它，就拿去吧。
43. 你能幫我一個忙嗎？
44. 如果你沒有鋼筆，鉛筆也可以。

(2) ─────────────────────────────────────── would 和 should

45. 以你希望受到的待遇去對待別人。
46. 丹過去常常一坐幾個小時，安靜並且心不在焉地，不注意任何人。

47. 我寧死也不過屈辱的生活。
48. 不管我們多用力，那門就是打不開。
49. 你不該抱怨老師沒有幫忙，你已經夠大，可以自己做了。

50. 音樂會非常成功。你應該和我們一塊兒去的。

───

"注意"　47. *would rather* = *would better* "寧願"　48. would not 表
過去的否定。　49. *complain of* "抱怨"　50.「 should have ＋ p.p. 」
表過去該做而沒做的事。

（ 3 ）————————————————————— can, may, must

51. Tom is such a kind man that he *cannot* have committed such cruelties.

52. Trouble *may* break out at any moment.

53. He *may have finished* the repairs by this time.

54. *May* God bless you !

55. He *may well* be proud of his son.

56. You *may as well* die *as* yield to force.

57. Every Jack *must* have his Jill.

58. Tom never breaks his promise. Something *must have happened* to him.

59. We *cannot* be *too* careful of our health.

60. Betty was so earnest that I *could not but* trust her.

〔註〕 51.「 cannot have ＋ p.p. 」表對過去事物否定的推測。*such ～ that …*
"如此～以致於…" 52. *break out* "發生" 53.「 may have ＋ p.p. 」表對過
去的猜測，可能性也許現在還沒消失。 54. May ～ ! "願～ !" 用於祈願句
中。cf. 615. 55. *may well ～* "理所當然～ ; 有足夠理由～" *be proud of*
= *take pride in* "以～為榮" 56. *may as well ～ as …* "與其…不如～"

（3）——————————————————————— can, may, must

51. 湯姆是一個這麼仁慈的人，不可能做這樣殘酷的行爲。

52. 麻煩隨時都可能發生。

53. 這個時候他可能已經做完修理的工作了。

54. 願上帝祝福你！

55. 他大可以他的兒子爲榮。

56. 你若向暴力屈服，不如死掉。

57. 人各有偶。〔諺〕

58. 湯姆從未食言。他一定發生了什麼事了。

59. 我們無論怎樣注意我們的健康也不爲過。

60. 貝蒂是那麼認眞，以致於我不得不相信她。

---

yield to ~ "向～屈服"　57. must ＋原形動詞　表對現在肯定的推測。
58.「must have ＋ p.p.」表對過去肯定的推測。*break one's promise*
"食言"　59. *cannot ~ too* … "再怎麼…也不爲過"　*be careful of* "小
心"　60. *cannot but* ＋V "不得不～"

(4) ─────────────────── used to, ought to, have to, need

61. There *used to* be some benches in this garden.

62. You *ought to* take pride in your background.

63. Such things *ought not to* be allowed at school.

64. You *ought not to have been* idle when young.

65. Do we *have to* change trains here?

66. If you want to make friends with him, you *have only to* speak to him.

67. I *need not* introduce strangers to each other at the party.

68. Jack *needn't have gone* to the doctor's every other day.

(5) ─────────────────────── dare, had better

69. How *dare* you say such things in my presence?

70. You *had better* take an umbrella in case it rains.

〔註〕 61. used to 表過去的習慣、狀態。 62. *ought to* ～ "應該～",有 should 的意味。 63. ought to 的否定形為 *ought not to* 64. 「ought to have ＋ p.p.」表過去該做而未做的事。 65. have to ＝ must, *change trains* "換火車" 66. *make friends with* ～ "跟～做朋友" 67. need not ＝ don't have to 68. 「needn't have ＋ p.p.」表過去不必做而已做

（4）──────────── used to, ought to, have to, need

61. 這個公園裏以前有些長板櫈。

62. 你應該以你的背景自豪。

63. 這樣的事在學校不該被允許。

64. 你年輕的時候不該懶惰。

65. 我們必須在這裏換火車嗎？

66. 如果你想跟他做朋友，你只要對他說就好了。

67. 在宴會上我不需介紹互不相識的客人。

68. 傑克不須每隔一天到診所去。

（5）──────────── dare, had better

69. 你怎敢在我面前說這種事情？

70. 你最好帶把傘以防萬一下雨。

──────────────────────────

的事。69. 不是眞正疑問句，而是對所做的事表示“憤怒、譴責”的意思。
in one's presence “當某人的面” 70. *had better* “最好”，表勸解或
間接命令。 *in case* “以防萬一”

4. Infinitive

（1）——————————————————— 不定詞的名詞用法（作主詞）

71. *To say* is one thing and *to practice* is another.
72. *It* is not always easy *to keep* one's temper.
73. *It* is impossible for me *to get* in touch with him.

（2）——————————————————— 不定詞的名詞用法（作受詞、補語）

74. I should like *to introduce* Mr. Lee to you.
75. I make *it* a rule *to take* a walk with my dog before breakfast.
76. All you have to do is (*to*)*fight* it out to the finish.

（3）——————————————————— 不定詞的形容詞用法

77. There is no paper *to write* on, nor any pen *to write* with.
78. The only sound *to be heard* was the ticking of the clock.
79. Bob is the last man *to do* such a thing.
80. It is time for us to make up our mind *to start* the work.

【註】71. ～ 73. 為不定詞作主詞。 It is ～（for …）to 一的形式，It 為形式主詞，不定詞才是真正主詞。 72. *keep one's temper* "忍住怒氣" 73. *get in touch with*～ "與～聯絡" 74. ～ 76. 為不定詞的名詞用法，作動詞或介詞的受詞或補語。 74. *introduce* A *to* B "介紹A給B" 75. it 為形式受詞，to take ～ 才是真正受詞。 *make it a rule to*～ "慣於～；照

4. 不　定　詞

71. 說是一回事，做又是一回事。──知易行難。〔格言〕
72. 要忍住怒氣未必是件容易的事。
73. 要我和他聯絡是不可能的。

74. 我想向你介紹李先生。
75. 我習慣在早餐前帶我的狗去散步。

76. 你所必須做的，就是把它做完。

77. 沒紙可寫，也沒筆可寫。

78. 唯一能聽到的，只是時鐘的滴嗒聲。

79. 鮑伯是最不可能做這種事的人。
80. 是我們下定決心開始工作的時候了。

例要～" 76. *fight it out to the finish* "戰到底；做到完" 77. ～ 80.
為不定詞的形容詞用法 77. 被修飾的名詞 paper，是不定詞意義上的受詞。
78. 79. 被修飾的名詞 sound, man，是不定詞意義上的主詞。 79. *the last*
＋名詞 "最不可能～的" 80. *make up one's mind* "下決心"

(4)——————————————————————— 不定詞的副詞用法

81. What do you think we Chinese must do *to maintain* the peace of the world?

82 Mr. Lin was pleased *to know* what to do with it.

83. You are stupid *to depend upon* such a dishonest person as he.

84. Hundreds of years ago few people lived *to be* seventy.

85. I tried again *only to fail*.

86. *To hear* Anny speak English, you might take her for an American.

(5)——————————————————————— 不定詞的格言用法

87. It is *never too* late *to mend*.

88. One is *never too* old *to learn*.

89. It takes all sorts *to make* a world.

90. It takes two *to make* a quarrel.

〔註〕81. ~ 86. 為不定詞的副詞用法。 81. 不定詞片語表目的 82. 表原因。不定詞跟在 glad, sorry, surprised 後表感情的原因。what to do with ~ "怎樣處理~" 83. 表理由。*depend upon* "依賴" 84. 85. 表結果。84. lived to be = lived until they were 85. *only to fail* = but failed. only to 表「令人失望的結果」。 86. To hear = If you hear 表

（4）———————————————————————— 不定詞的副詞用法

81. 你認爲我們中國人必須維持世界和平嗎？

82. 林先生很高興知道怎樣處理它。

83. 你信賴像他這麼一個不誠實的人，眞是愚蠢。

84. 數百年前很少人能活到七十歲。

85. 我再嘗試，結果還是失敗。

86. 聽安妮說英語，你會以爲她是美國人。

（5）———————————————————————— 不定詞的格言用法

87. 改過自新永不嫌遲；亡羊補牢，爲時未晚。

88. 活到老，學到老。

89. 世界是由各式各樣的人組成的。

90. 兩個人才能吵架；一個碗不響。

條件。 cf. 320. *take ～ for* …「以爲～是…」 87. ～ 90. 爲不定詞的格言
用法。格言、諺語最好熟背。 87. *too ～ to* … "太～以致於無法…"
90. *make a quarrel* "吵架"

（6）————————————————————— 接在形容詞後面的不定詞

91. Robert is *slow to learn*.

92. He is *eager to try* anything new.

93. He is *easy to deal with*. You have only to get a box of chocolate for him.

94. She is *certain to win* the first prize in the speech contest.

95. This river is *dangerous to swim* in.

96. It is said that Japanese universities are *difficult to get* into, but *easy to graduate* from.

97. Jane is *sure to do* the work in your place.

（7）————————————————————— 獨立不定詞

98. *To do him justice*, he did his best with his limited supplies.

99. *To tell the truth*, I am at a loss which way to go.

100. *To begin with*, we are going to do shopping at the supermarket.

〔註〕91. ～ 97. 接在形容詞後面的不定詞，可以用 It 為主詞的句子來代換。 92. *be eager to* "渴望" 93. = It is easy to deal with him. *deal with* "相處" 94. = It is certain that she will win the first prize …
95. = It is dangerous to swim in this river. 96. = It is difficult to get into Japanese university, but easy to graduate from them.

（ 6 ）————————————————— 接在形容詞後面的不定詞

91. 羅伯特學習遲鈍。
92. 他渴望去嘗試任何新的東西。
93. 他很容易相處。你只要買盒巧克力給他。

94. 她一定會贏得演講比賽第一名。

95. 在這條河裏游泳很危險。
96. 據說日本大學很難進去，但是很容易畢業。

97. 珍一定會代替你做那工作。

（ 7 ）————————————————————— 獨立不定詞

98. 平心而論，他以他有限的資力，盡了最大的努力。

99. 說實話，我不知道要走哪條路。
100. 首先，我們要到超級市場買東西。

---

97. *in one's place* "代替某人" 98. ～100. 獨立不定詞可說是副詞片語，修飾全句。其他例子：*to be frank with you* "老實跟你說"，*strange to say* "說也奇怪" 98. *To do one justice* "對～給予公平的評價" 99. *to tell the truth* "說老實話" 100. *To begin with* "首先" *do shopping* "買東西"

(8)──────────────────────────────── 含不定詞的慣用語

101. Henry was forced into this business at the age of ten *in order to* help his father.

102. A house should be built *so as to admit* plenty of light.

103. She is *too* stubborn *to admit* her faults.

104. He was *kind enough to provide* me *with* the food.

105. He was *so kind as to provide* me *with* the food.

(9)──────────────────────────────── 動詞＋不定詞

106. Nowadays a large number of young people *have come to travel* abroad.

107. A speech to the people *is to be made* by the President over television.

108. No matter how busy I was, I *never failed to answer* your letters.

109. He *seems to have made* a mistake.

110. He *intended to have had* his own way, but was prevented from doing so.

【註】101. 和 102. *in order to* ～ = *so as to* ～ "爲了～" 103. = She is *so* stubborn *that* she *can't* admit her faults. 104. *provide* A *with* B "把 B 供給 A" 105. = He kindly provided me with the food. 106. *come to* "變成" 108. never fail to ～ = always ～ 109. seem to have + p.p. 表示發生在主要動詞之前的動作。此句 = It *seems* that

（8）————————————————————————— 含不定詞的慣用語

101. 亨利爲了幫助他父親，十歲就被迫進入這一行。

102. 建一棟房子應該要採光良好。

103. 她太固執了，不可能承認她的過失。

104. 他很仁慈，供給我食物。

105. 他很仁慈，供給我食物。

（9）————————————————————————————— 動詞＋不定詞

106. 目前很多年輕人到國外旅行。

107. 總統透過電視對人民發表一場演講。

108. 不管我有多忙，從不會忘記給你回信。

109. 他似犯了錯。

110. 他想隨心所欲，不過被阻止了。

---

he *made* a mistake.　110. intend 和 mean 的過去式之後接完成式不定詞，
表過去沒有實現的希望、計畫等（詳見文法寶典 p.339, p.423）　***have one's
own way*** "隨心所欲；爲所欲爲"

(10) ———————————— It is ～ of … to －, S+V+O+ to 的句型

111. *It was wise of* him *not to accept* the offer.

112. *His mother asked me to make* a real magician of him.

113. *I advised* Elizabeth *not to attend* the meeting.

(11) ———————————————————— 原形不定詞

114. I *heard* Jack *call* out for help.

115. Dorothy *had* her mother *make* a new dress.

116. Don't *let* him *make* a trip by himself.

117. At first I *made* him *do* the task against his will.

118. Why not *join* us ?

119. The baby *did nothing but cry* and I did not know what to do with it.

120. I *could not but admire* his skill in handwork.

【註】 111. = He was wise not to accept the offer.　112. 和 113. 的形式 ask, advise, teach, tell, expect, order, request, allow 等動詞後面常接不定詞做受詞補語（詳見文法寶典 p.437）　112. *make* A *of* B "使 B 成爲 A"　114. 感官動詞（hear, see, feel, observe 等）後接原形不定詞作受詞補語。*call out* "大叫"　115. ～117. 使役動詞（make, let, have, bid 等）後

（10）────────── It is ～ of … to － , S＋V＋O＋to 的句型

111. 他不接受那項提議，是明智的。

112. 他的母親要求我把他訓練成一個眞正的魔術師。

113. 我勸伊莉莎白不要參加那會議。

（11）──────────────────────── 原形不定詞

114. 我聽傑克大喊救命。

115. 朶勒絲叫她的母親做一件新衣服。

116. 不要讓他一個人去旅行。

117. 首先我要他做違背意志的工作。

118. 何不加入我們？

119. 這嬰孩就只會哭，我不知道要拿他怎麼辦才好。

120. 我不得不稱讚他手工的技巧。

接原形不定詞作受詞補語。　116. *make a trip* "旅行"　*by oneself* "獨自"
117. *against one's will* "違背某人意志"　118.「why not ＋原形動詞」
在口語中用來向對方提出勸告。　119. *do nothing but* "只是"
120. *cannot but* "不得不"

5. Gerund

（1）———————————————————————— 動名詞的基本用法

121. *Saying* is one thing and *doing* another.
122. Do you *mind telling* me the truth?
123. Nick has been *looking forward to seeing* you again.
124. *What do you say to going* to the concert tonight?
125. As a whole they *are used to living* in such a high place.
126. *Besides being* sleepy, she was a little feverish.

（2）———————————————————————— 動名詞意義上的主詞

127. Peter insisted on *my paying* the bill.
128. Never complain of the *room being* too small.

（3）———————————————————————— 動名詞的時式和語態

129. The witness *denied having seen* the accused.
130. Barbara *needed looking after*.

【註】123.～125. 的 to 都是介系詞，所以後面接動名詞。　123. *look forward to+V-ing* "盼望～"　124. *What do you say to+V-ing* "你要不要～"
125. *as a whole* "總而言之"　*be used to+V-ing* "習慣於～"
126. ＝She was not only sleepy, but also a little feverish.
127. ＝Peter insisted that I（*should*）pay the bill.　*insist on+*

5. 動 名 詞

（1）———————————————————— 動名詞的基本用法

121. 說是一回事，做又是一回事；說來容易做來難。

122. 你介意告訴我實話嗎？

123. 尼克一直盼望再見到你。

124. 你今晚要不要去聽音樂會？

125. 總而言之，他們習慣住在這麼高的地方。

126. 除了想睡以外，她還有點發燒。

（2）———————————————————— 動名詞意義上的主詞

127. 彼得堅持我付賬。

128. 決不要抱怨這房間太小。

（3）———————————————————— 動名詞的時式和語態

129. 那目擊者否認看過被告。

130. 芭芭拉需要照料。

V-ing "堅持～" 128. *complain of* "抱怨" 129.完成式的動名詞，表示比主要動詞先發生的動作或狀態。 the accused "被告" 130. need, want 作"需要"解時，後接主動形式的動名詞，表示被動的意思。 need looking after ＝ need to be looked after

(4) ——————————————————————————— 含動名詞的慣用語

131. *On arriving* at the station, I called my uncle in order to ask him the way to his house.

132. *In entering* the room something curious will catch your eye.

133. Grace was so funny that I *could not help laughing*.

134. When I was left alone in the dark room, I *felt like crying*.

135. *It goes without saying* that there is no place like home.

136. *It is no use crying* over spilt milk.

137. *There is no accounting* for tastes.

138. *If* a thing is *worth doing*, it is *worth doing* well.

139. I *never* see you *without thinking* of my father.

140. Winston showed me a picture *of his own painting*.

【註】131. On arriving＝As soon as I arrived　132. In entering＝When you enter　*catch one's eye* "吸引某人注意"　133. *cannot help*＋ *V-ing＝cannot but*＋*V*　134. *feel like*＋*V-ing* "想～"　135. *It goes without saying that* "不用說～"　136. *It is no use*＋*V-ing* "～是沒用的"　137. *There is no*＋*V-ing* "沒有～" 此句＝It is

（4）———————————————————— 含動名詞的慣用語

131. 我一到達車站就打電話給我叔叔，問到他家的路。

132. 一進到那房間，有個奇怪的東西將會吸引你的注意。

133. 葛瑞絲看起來那麼滑稽，使得我忍不住發笑。

134. 當我一個人被留在那黑暗的房間時，我好想哭。

135. 不用說，沒有地方像家一樣。

136. 覆水難收。〔諺〕

137. 品味無可爭論。——人各有好。〔諺〕

138. 如果一件事值得做，就值得將它做好。——凡事當盡其完美。〔諺〕

139. 我每次看到你都會想到我父親。

140. 溫斯頓拿一張他自己畫的圖畫給我看。

---

impossible to account for tastes. *or* We can't account for tastes.
account for "說明" 138. ***worth*** + ***V-ing*** "值得～" 139. = Whenever
I see you, I think of my father. 140. = He showed me a picture
that he had painted for himself.

6. Participle

(1) ──────────────────────────────── 現在分詞作形容詞

141. *Barking dogs* seldom bite.

142. A *drowning man* will catch at a straw.

143. Let *sleeping dogs* lie.

144. A *rolling stone* gathers no moss.

145. The *lady preparing* dinner in the kitchen is not my mother, but my aunt.

(2) ──────────────────────────────── 過去分詞作形容詞

146. A *burnt child* dreads the fire.

147. The *lost chance* will never come again.

148. The lady is always dressed in good taste. She is probably a *cultured lady*.

149. The *lady dressed* in white is my aunt.

150. What is the *language spoken* on that island?

【註】 141.~144.分詞單獨修飾名詞時，放在所修飾名詞前面。 142. *catch at* "抓住" 145. 現在分詞有受詞或修飾片語時，放在所修飾名詞的後面。

146.~148. 過去分詞單獨修飾名詞時，放在所修飾名詞的前面。 146. 相似的諺語有：Once bitten, twice shy. (一回上當二回乖；上一次當，學一次

6. 分　詞

141. 會叫的狗不咬人；色厲內荏。〔諺〕

142. 快淹死的人連一根草都會抓住；急不暇擇。〔諺〕

143 讓睡覺的狗躺著；勿惹事生非；勿打草驚蛇。〔諺〕

144. 轉石不生苔；轉業不聚財。〔諺〕

145. 正在厨房準備晚飯的女士，不是我媽媽，而是我舅母。

146. 灼傷過的小孩怕火；一朝被蛇咬，十年怕草繩。〔諺〕

147. 失去的機會不會再來。

148. 那位女士總是穿得很高尚。她大概是位有教養的女士。

149. 那位穿白色衣服的女士是我的舅母。

150. 在那島上說什麼語言？

乖。）　148. *in good taste* "高尚"　149. 和 150. 過去分詞有受詞或修飾片語時，放在所修飾的名詞後面。

（ 3 ）———————————————— 現在分詞當補語

151. Tom *came running* out of the room.

152. The truck broke down and it was morning before I could *get it going*.

153. Contrary to my expectations, I *heard Betty and John quarreling* when I came back from my work.

154. I was *kept waiting* by him for such a long time that I missed the 10:00 a.m. train.

155. I had *some difficulty* (in) *solving* the problem.

156. She *spent much of her spare time* (in) *window-shopping* downtown.

（ 4 ）———————————————— 過去分詞當補語

157. All the windows of the house *remained closed* all day long.

158. Mary *left the door unlocked*.

159. I was so tired that I wanted to *have my baggage carried* to my room.

160. I spoke slowly and clearly so as to *make myself understood* in Chinese.

【 註 】 151. S ＋ V ＋ V-ing 的句型，動詞多為 come, go, lie, stand, sit, keep 等。 152. ～ 154. 是 S ＋ V ＋ O ＋ V-ing 的句型。 *break down* " 故障；拋錨 " 154. 是被動語態。須接分詞作受詞補語的動詞多為（a）感官動詞（b）使役動詞（have , make 等） （c） find, keep, leave。

(3)————————————————————— 現在分詞當補語

151. 湯姆從房間跑了出來 。

152. 卡車拋錨了，等我把它發動時，已經是早上了 。

153. 當我工作回來時，聽到貝蒂和約翰正在吵架，這和我預期的正好相反 。

154. 我等他等了好久好久，以致於錯過了早上十點的那班火車 。

155. 解決這問題，我有點困難 。

156. 她花了大半餘暇到商業區逛街 。

(4)————————————————————— 過去分詞當補語

157. 那棟房子的所有窗戶整天都關著 。

158. 瑪麗沒關門 。

159. 我很疲倦，因此我要人把我的行李搬到我的房間去 。

160 我慢慢地，清楚地說，使我的中文能被了解 。

---

155. 和 156. 加 in 時 V-ing 視爲動名詞，不加 in 時視爲現在分詞 。

156. *spare time* "餘暇" 157. S＋V＋p.p. 的句型，動詞多爲appear, feel, lie, remain 等。*all day long* "整天" 160. *so as to*＋V "以便～" *make oneself understood* "使人了解自己的話"

（5）——————————————————————— 現在分詞的分詞構句

161. *Standing* on the hill, his house commands a fine view.
162. *Turning* to the right at the second crossing, you will find the post office.
163. *Admitting* what you say is right, I still object to your plan.
164. *Making* use of his knowledge, man has succeeded in creating something marvelous in a short time.
165. *Not knowing* what to do, I asked for his advice.

（6）——————————————————————— 完成式的分詞構句

166. *Having met* him before, I noticed him at once.
167. *Having written* my exercises, I have nothing more to do.

（7）——————————————————————— 過去分詞的分詞構句

168. *Left* to herself, Emily burst into tears.
169. *Printed* in haste, the book has lots of misprints.
170. *Seen* from a distance, the mountain looks like a horse.

【註】以分詞爲中心，修飾主要子句全句的片語，稱爲分詞構句。 161. ＝Since it stands … *command a fine view* "俯瞰美景" 162. ＝If you turn to … 163. ＝Though I admit … *object to* "反對" 164. ＝Man made use of his knowledge and … *make use of* "利用" 165. 分詞的否定形，not 放在分詞前面。 166. 和 167. 所表示的時間比主要

（5）————————————————————— 現在分詞的分詞構句

161. 他的房子因位在山丘上，所以能俯瞰美景。
162. 在第二個十字路口向右轉，你就會看到郵局。

163. 雖然我承認你說的對，不過還是反對你的計畫。

164. 人類利用了知識，成功地在短時間內創造了不可思議的事物。

165. 因爲我不知道該怎麼辦，因此要求他給我忠告。

（6）————————————————————— 完成式的分詞構句

166. 因爲以前見過他，我立刻注意到他。
167. 因爲功課都做完了，我沒事可做。

（7）————————————————————— 過去分詞的分詞構句

168. 因爲一個人給留下來，愛彌莉突然大哭起來。
169. 由於印刷匆促，這本書有許多地方印錯了。
170. 如果從遠處看，那座山就像一隻馬。

子句的動詞早完成。　166. = As I had met him before …　167. = As I have written …　168. ~ 170. 在被動態中的 being 或 having been 可省略。 168. = As she was left …　*leave sb. to oneself* "把某人獨自留下" *burst into tears* "突然大哭"　169. = As the book was printed in haste …　170. = When it is seen …

（8）────────────────────────────── 獨立分詞構句

171. *There being* no bus service, we had to walk all the way to the hotel.

172. *The sun having risen*, they continued their journey.

173. *This work done*, we went home.

（9）──────────────────────「 with ＋受詞＋分詞 」的型式

174. Tom rushed out of the room *with his eyes shining*.

175. *With his friends helping*, he finished the job in a week.

176. He thought the matter over *with his arms folded*.

177. He walked *with his eyes fixed* on the ground.

（10）──────────────────────── 含分詞的慣用語

178. *Generally speaking*, this essay is not so pessimistic about the future.

179. *Judging from* the look of the sky, it will rain in the afternoon.

180. *Granting* what he said, it will not enable us to over-come the present situation.

──

【註】171. ～ 173. 當分詞構句的意義上的主詞，不是句子的主詞時，必須在分詞構句前保留意義上的主詞，此種帶有意義主詞的分詞結構與主要子句主詞無文法關聯，所以稱為獨立分詞構句。 171. ＝ Since there was no bus service, … *all the way* "老遠地" 172. ＝ As the sun had risen, … 173. ＝ As this work was done, … 174.～177. with ＋O＋分詞；表附帶

(8)──────────────────────── 獨立分詞構句

171. 由於沒有汽車運輸，我們必須老遠地走到旅館去。

172. 當太陽升起，他們就繼續旅行。

173. 這個工作一做好，我們就回家。

(9)──────────────────────「with＋受詞＋分詞」的型式

174. 湯姆帶著閃耀的眼神，突然跑出房間。

175. 藉著他朋友的幫助，他在一星期之內完成了工作。

176. 他交叉著兩臂考慮那件事。

177. 他兩眼盯著地面走路。

(10)──────────────────────含分詞的慣用語

178. 一般而言，這篇文章對未來不那麼悲觀。

179. 從天色看來，下午將會下雨。

180. 就算他說的是對的，我們也不能夠克服現在的情況。

狀態。 176. *think over*「考慮」 177. *fix one's eyes on*～ "兩眼盯
著～看" 178.～180. 有些獨立分詞意義上的主詞表示「一般人」時，主詞
可以省略。 178. *generally speaking* "一般而言" 179. *judging from*～
"從～判斷"

7. Subjunctive

（1）——————————————————————————— 與現在事實相反的假設

181. *If* I *were* a teacher, I *would* not *give* any assignments during the summer vacation.
182. *If* Jack *were* well off, he *would* not *depend* upon us any longer.
183. *I wish* I *were* as smart as he is.
184. *If only* there *were* no earthquakes in the world.
185. *It's time* we *went* to bed.

（2）——————————————————————————— 與過去事實相反的假設

186. *If* we *had had* enough time, we *could have been* to the concert.
187. *If* you *had asked* him politely, Father *wouldn't have objected* to your using his car.
188. *If* the war *hadn't broken* out, we *would be married* and *be* happy now.
189. *If* I *had been* more careful, I *might not be* in trouble now.
190. *I wish* I *had looked* into the matter more carefully.

【註】181. 和 182. 爲與現在事實相反的假設，公式爲「If＋S＋過去式（或
were）～，S＋would（should, could, might）＋原形動詞」 182. *be*
well off "富有" 183. 和 184. 爲與現在事實相反的願望，公式爲「I
wish＋S＋過去式或were」或「If only＋S＋過去式或were」
186. 和 187. 爲與過去事實相反的假設，公式爲「If＋S＋過去完成式～，

7. 假 設 法

（ 1 ）───────────────────── 與現在事實相反的假設

181. 如果我是個老師，暑假期間一定不出任何作業。

182. 如果傑克富有的話，他就再也不會依賴我們了。

183. 眞希望我跟他一樣聰明。
184. 世界上要是沒有地震就好了。
185. 是我們該上床睡覺的時候了。

（ 2 ）───────────────────── 與過去事實相反的假設

186. 如果我們當時有時間的話，就可以去參加音樂會了。

187. 如果你當時禮貌地要求，父親就不會反對你用他的車子了。

188. 如果戰爭沒有爆發的話，我們已經結了婚，正過著快樂的生活。

189. 如果當時我更小心的話，現在就不會有麻煩了。

190. 眞希望我當時更小心地調查那件事情。

S＋would（should, could, might）＋have＋過去分詞」。 188. 和 189.
「 如果（過去）…，（現在）就～」是與現在事實相反的假設。188. *break
out* “ 爆發 ” 189. *be in trouble* “ 處於困難中 ” 190. 爲與過去事實
相反的願望，公式爲「 I wish ＋S＋過去完成式」或「 If only ＋S＋過去
完成式 」

（3）―――――――――――――――――― **should** 和 **were to** 的假設

191. *If* Dick *were to* give you a million dollars, what *would* you *do* with it?

192. *Even if* you *were to* try all night, you *would* never *guess* the answer to the riddle.

193. *If* a third world war *should break out*, it *would bring about* the extermination of mankind.

194. I'll be back soon, but *if* he *should come* in my absence, tell him I have no objection to his plan.

（4）―――――――――――――――――― 應注意的假設法句型

195. You *talk as if* you *knew* him in person.

196. You *talked as if* you *knew* him in person.

197. Anne *is* out of breath *as if* she *had been running*.

198. Anne *was* out of breath *as if* she *had been running*.

199. *If it were not for* traffic accidents, people *would be* happier.

200. *If it had not been for* your encouragement and aid, I *would have given up* going to college.

【註】191. 和 192. were to 表示未來絕對不可能 192. *even if* "即使" 193.和 194. should 表可能性極小。 194. *in one's absence* "某人不在時" *have no objection to ~* "不反對~" 195. ~ 198. 由 as if "好像" 所 引導的子句的時式，不受主要子句影響。 195. *in person* "本人"

(3)———————————————————————— should 和 were to 的假設

191. 如果狄克給你一百萬元，你要怎麼用它？

192. 即使你想一整晚，你也想不出這道謎語的解答。

193. 如果第三次世界大戰爆發，將會給人類帶來毀滅。

194. 我馬上會回來，不過如果他在我不在時來了，告訴他我不反對他的計畫。

(4)———————————————————————— 應注意的假設法句型

195. 你說話的樣子，就好像你本人認識他似的。
196. 你當時說話的樣子，就好像你本人認識他似的。
197. 安妮喘不過氣來，好像是跑著到這裏似的。
198. 安妮喘不過氣來，好像跑過似的。
199. 如果沒有交通事故的話，人們會快樂一點。

200. 如果不是你的鼓勵和幫助，我就放棄上大學了。

---

197. *be out of breath* "喘不過氣" 199. *If it were not for ～* "如果不是因爲～的話"意思和 But for ～同。 200. If it had not been for ～ "如果（當時）不是～的話"，也可用 But for ～代換。*give up* "放棄"

（5）――――――――――――――――――――――――――――― 相當於 **if** 子句的語句

201. A *man of common sense* in general would not say such a thing in public.
202. A *brave man* would have acted differently.
203. *Without* the light and heat of the sun, what would become of all the animals on earth?
204. *But for* her help, I would have lost my way.
205. *With* a little more effort, you would have passed the entrance examination.
206. The traffic was very heavy; *otherwise* I would have been here much sooner.

（6）――――――――――――――――――――――――――――― 省略了 **if** 的假設法

207. *Were it not for* the scholarship, I could not come to college.
208. *Were it not for* his idleness, I would employ him.
209. *Had it not been for* the money his father left him, he would have failed in his business.
210. *Should it rain* tomorrow, the picnic will be put off.

―――

【註】201. 和 202. 名詞片語中含假設意味。 201. *in general* "一般而言" *in public* "在公共場合" 203. 和 204. Without ～和 But for ～ 等介詞片語中含假設意味。 203. *become of* "遭遇" 204. *lose one's way* "迷失方向" 205. with～變爲假設意味的介詞片語。 206. otherwise ＝ if the

（5）———————————————————— 相當於 **if** 子句的語句

201. 通常一個有常識的人，不會在公共場合說這種事。

202. 一個勇敢的人會有不同的表現。

203. 如果沒有太陽的光和熱，地球上所有的動物將會變成怎樣？

204. 若不是有她的幫忙，我就迷失了方向了。

205. 如果你再多努力一些，就會通過入學考試了。

206. 當時交通非常擁擠；否則我會更快地到達這裏。

（6）———————————————————— 省略了 **if** 的假設法

207. 若不是有獎學金，我就不能進大學了。

208. 若不是因為他懶惰，我會雇用他。

209. 若不是有他父親留給他的錢，他的事業早就失敗了。

210. 萬一明天下雨的話，野餐將要延期。

---

traffic had not been very heavy. 假設語氣中，表條件的副詞子句的 if
可以省略，但主詞與助動詞必須易位。　207. 和 208. = If it were not
for … 　209. = If it had not been for … ，*fail in* "失敗"
210. = If it should rain … 　*put off* "延期"

8. It & There

（1）———————————————————— it 可表天氣、時間、距離等狀況

211. *It* never rains but it pours.

212. Since the rainy season set in, *it* has been raining off and on for nearly a month.

213. " How far is *it* from here to the post office ? " " *It* is about ten minutes' walk. "

214. *It* is five years since I came to live in Taipei.

215. *It* was ten years before I came back to my home town.

216. *It* was not long before I heard of Linda.

217. You are ten minutes behind. How long does *it take* you to catch up with them ?

218. *It takes* me five minutes to walk to the station.

219. Take *it* easy.

220. *It* is all over with me.

【註】 211. ~ 220. it 可表天氣、時間、距離等。 211. 和 212. 指天氣狀況。
212. *set in* "開始" *off and on* "斷斷續續" 213. *ten minutes'*
walk "十分鐘的路程" 此種表距離的用法還有：*a stone's throw* "一
石之遙" *a hair's breadth* "千鈞一髮" 214. ~ 216. 指時間。 215. It
was ten years before ~ = After ten years' absence ~ 216. *hear of*

8. It和There的句型

（1）───────────────── **it** 可表天氣、時間、距離等狀況

211. 不雨則已，一雨傾盆；屋漏偏逢連夜雨；禍不單行。〔諺〕

212. 自從雨季開始，已經斷斷續續下了快一個月的雨了。

213. "從這裏到郵局多遠？" "大概有十分鐘的路程。"

214. 我住在台北五年了。

215. 過了十年我才回到我的家鄉。

216. 不久前我才聽到林達的消息。

217. 你落後了十分鐘。你多久才趕上他們的？

218. 我走到車站要五分鐘。

219. 別緊張。

220. 我完了。

"聽到" *not long before* "不久前"　217. 和 218. It takes～ "花了～時間"　217. *catch up with* "趕上"　218. 此句的 take 爲授與動詞。可改爲 It takes five minutes for me to walk… 此時的 take 不是授與動詞。

(2) ——————————————————————————— It ～ to …的句型

221 *It* cost Robert twenty thousand dollars *to have* his house repaired.

222. *It* is next to impossible *to work* five days on end without sleeping.

223. *It* was kind of you *to warn* me against the danger.

(3) ——————————————————————————— It ～ that …的句型

224. *It* is a matter for regret *that* young people forget their manners.

225. Since I was born and brought up in the States, *it* is natural *that* I should speak fluent English.

226. *It* is no wonder *that* he has failed in his business.

227. *It* is a pity *that* you have to stay in bed for a week and cannot come with us.

(4) ——————————————————————————— It ～ whether …的句型

228. *It* is doubtful *whether* his words are true or not.

229. *It* does not make much difference *whether* Jane is responsible for it or not

230. *It* matters little *whether* you go by bus or by train.

【註】 221.～223. It ～ to …的構句中，It 為形式主詞，不定詞才是眞正主詞。
221. have＋*sth.*＋p.p. "使某物～" 222. *next to impossible* "幾乎
不可能" *on end* "繼續地" 223. ＝You were kind enough to warn
me against the danger. 224.～227. It ～ that …的構句中，It 為形式
主詞，that 子句為眞正主詞。其形式為「 It＋V＋C＋ that 子句」

（2）──────────────────────── It ～ to …的句型

221. 羅勃特花了兩萬元修補他的房子。

222. 連續工作五天不睡覺，幾乎是不可能的。

223. 你真好，警告我注意危險。

（3）──────────────────────── It ～ that …的句型

224. 年輕人忘了他們的禮節是件憾事。

225 因為我生長在美國，自然能說流利的英文。

226. 難怪他生意失敗。

227. 真是可惜，你必須在床上躺一個禮拜，不能跟我們一起去。

（4）──────────────────────── It ～ whether …的句型

228. 他的話是否是真的，難以確定。

229. 珍是否要對這件事負責，並沒有太大的關係。

230. 你搭公共汽車或是搭火車去，都沒什麼關係。

──────────────────────────────

224. a matter for regret "憾事"　*225. bring up* "教養"　*227. stay in bed = be in bed* "在床上"　*228. ～ 230.* It ～ whether …的構句中，It 為形式主詞，whether 子句為真正主詞。其形式為「 It ＋ V ＋ C（或O）＋ whether 子句」或「 It ＋ V（＋副詞片語）＋ whether 子句」　*229. be responsible for* "對～負責"

（5）———————————————————————— it 當形式受詞

231. We all thought *it* impossible *to travel* across the desert without a car.

232. I make *it* a rule *to take* exercise before breakfast.

233. I found *it* pleasant *working* with such nice people.

234. I took *it* for granted *that* he would accept my offer.

235. I owe *it* to you *that* I have succeeded.

236. See to *it that* the baby is taken good care of.

（6）———————————————————————— It seems that ～ 的句型

237. *It seems that* Anne is ashamed of her deed.

238. *It seems that* he devoted himself to his studies.

239. *It appears* to me *that* he has worked out a solution to his problems.

240. *It happened that* I was free that afternoon.

【註】 231.～236. it 當形式受詞。 231. 和 232. it 爲形式受詞，不定詞（片語）
才是眞正的受詞。 232. *make it a rule to* ～ "慣於～" *take exercise*
"運動" 233. 動名詞片語 working with such nice people 爲眞正受詞。
234.～236. that 子句爲眞正受詞，此類句型動詞多爲 think, find, make。
235. *owe* ～ *to* … "把～歸功於…" 236. *see to* ～ "留意～" 237.～

（5）───────────────────────────── it 當形式受詞

231. 我們都認爲，沒車子要橫渡沙漠旅行是不可能的。

232. 我習慣在早餐以前做運動。

233. 我發覺和這樣親切的人們一起工作，是令人愉快的。

234. 我認爲他會接受我的提議是理所當然的。

235. 我的成功要歸功於你。

236. 注意要好好照顧嬰兒。

（6）───────────────────────────── It seems that ～ 的句型

237. 安似乎爲她的行爲感到羞恥。

238. 他似乎專心於學業。

239. 依我看，他似乎想出了解決問題的方法了。

240. 那天下午我剛好有空。

───────────────────────────────

240. It seems that ～ 的句型中，it 爲形式主詞，that 子句爲眞正主詞。此句型除了 seem 以外，還常用 appear, happen, chance 等動詞。

237. = Anne seems to be ashamed of her deed. *be ashamed of ～* "以～爲恥" 238. = He seems to have devoted himself to his studies. *devote oneself to* "專心於" 239. *work out* "解決"

（7）——————————————————— It is ～ that … 的強調句型

241. *It is an ill wind that* blows nobody any good.
242. *It was Tom who* made fun of me.
243. *It is by reading good books that* we can keep up with the times.
244. *Who is it that* is standing at the end of the platform?

（8）——————————————————— There ～ 的句型

245. Suddenly *there came* a knock at the door.
246. *There is* no smoke without fire.
247. *There were* many people waiting for the door to be opened.
248. *There were* a lot of houses destroyed by the gas explosion.
249. You have done your best. *There is* no need for you to apologize.
250. *There is* no doubt that Dick will take over his father's business.

【註】 241. ～ 244. It is ＋所要加强的部分。 242. 爲 Tom made fun of me
的强調句，因指人，可用who代替that。 243. *keep up with* "趕上"
244. 爲Who is standing at the end of the platform? 的强調句。 cf.
671. ～ 678. 245. there 的後面用表示存在（live），來往（come），發
生（happen），狀態（seem）等不及物動詞。「 there be ～ 」的句型可用

(7)———————————————————————————— **It is ~ that** … 的强調句型

241. 世上不吹對人都無益的風；凡事皆有利有弊。〔 諺 〕

242. 取笑我的人就是湯姆。

243. 藉著讀好書，我們才能趕上時代。

244. 站在講台邊的人是誰？

(8)———————————————————————————— **There ~** 的句型

245. 突然間 有敲門的 聲音。

246. 無火不生煙；無風不起浪。〔 諺 〕

247. 有很多人正在等開門。

248. 有很多房子被瓦斯爆炸所摧毁。

249. 你已經盡了力了，沒必要去道歉。

250. 無可置疑地，狄克將接管他父親的事業。

---

see, hear, have 等動詞的句子代換。 247. = I saw many people waiting
for the door to be opened. 249. *There is no need~* " 沒~的必要"
250. *There is no doubt ~* " 無可置疑~" *take over* " 接管"

9. Relative

（1）──────────────────────── 關係代名詞 who, whose, whom

251. Heaven helps *those who* help themselves.
252. Mr. Smith is *the man who* I think is responsible for the safety of the children.
253. Mr. Smith is *the man (whom)* I think to be responsible for the safety of the children.
254. I have nothing to do with *the man (whom)* you are trying to get in touch with.
255. *The man with whom* I talked was in charge of the arrangement for the conference.
256. No matter how diligent he was, she did not hire *a man whose* past was unknown.
257. It seems far from easy to find *a woman who* is beautiful and *whose* speech is attractive as well.
258. A man is known by *the company* he keeps.

（2）──────────────────────── 關係代名詞 which

259. We are running out of money. *The work which* calls for a lot of money cannot be carried on.
260. This is *the dictionary (which)* I cannot do without when I go abroad.

【註】 251.～258. 先行詞爲人時，關係代名詞用 who, whose, whom　252. I think 爲插入語。 *be responsible for ～* "負責"　254. *have nothing to do with ～* "與～無關"　*get in touch with ～* "和～聯絡"
255. ＝ The man (*whom*) I talked with …　*in charge of* "負責"
257. *far from* "一點兒也不"　*as well* "亦；也"　258. the company

9. 關 係 詞

(1)───────────────── 關係代名詞 who, whose, whom

251. 天助自助者。〔諺〕

252. 我想史密斯先生就是負責孩子們安全的人。

253. 我想史密斯先生就是負責孩子們安全的人。

254. 我和那位你一直嘗試要聯絡上的人沒有關係。

255. 跟我說話的那個人負責那次會議的籌備。

256. 不管他有多勤奮,她也不會雇用一個來歷不明的人。

257. 要找一個又漂亮,談吐又吸引人的女人似乎很不容易。

258. 觀其友得知其人。〔諺〕

(2)───────────────── 關係代名詞 which

259. 我們錢快用完了。需要很多錢的這件工作無法繼續進行。

260. 這是一本我出國時少不了的字典。

---

that he keeps 的關係代名詞 that 省略。 259.～260. 人以外的先行詞可用 which。whom 和 which 當受詞時可省略。 259. *run out of* "用完" *call for* = require "需要" *carry on* "繼續進行" 260. *do without* ～ "缺乏～而過"

(3)──────────────────────────── 關係代名詞 that

261. *Who that* has common sense would break into the bank
to get money ?

262. *The man and dog that* fell into the river were saved
by the policeman.

263. John Williams is one of *the greatest composers that*
America has ever produced.

264. *All that* glitters is not *gold.*

(4)──────────────────────────── 關係代名詞的補述用法

265. The man who persuaded me to undergo an operation
was my *uncle, who* was a famous doctor.

266. The doctor gave me *some medicine, which* had no
effect on me.

267. My uncle bought me *a bag of candies,* some of *which*
I brought home for my little sister.

268. We reached *the hotel,* from *whose* balcony we could
look down at the town.

269. *Jane wanted to be independent of her parents, which*
made them angry.

270. *I was told to go there by subway , which* advice I
followed.

【註】 261. ～ 264. 先行詞是「人」或「非人」時，可用 that 代替 who 和 which。
261. *common sense* "常識" *break into* "闖入" 263. 先行詞有最高
級時用 that。 264. 先行詞有 all, very, only 等字時多用 that。 265. ～
270. 人或物的補述多用 who 或 which。

（3）——————————————————————————— 關係代名詞 that

261. 有常識的人誰會闖進銀行搶錢？

262. 跌入河流的那個人和狗，被警察救起來了。

263. 約翰・威廉斯是美國最偉大的作家之一。

264. 閃爍者未必是金；中看未必中用；人不可貌相。〔諺〕

（4）——————————————————————————— 關係代名詞的補述用法

265. 那個勸我接受手術的人是我叔叔，他是位有名的醫師。

266. 醫師給了我一些藥，它們對我無效。

267. 我叔叔買給我一袋糖果，其中有一些我帶回家給我妹妹。

268. 我們到達那家旅館，從它的陽台我們可以俯視此鎮。

269. 珍不想依賴父母生活，她父母對這件事非常生氣。

270. 有人告訴我坐地下鐵去那裏，我遵照了那項勸告。

---

265. *persuade ～ to* … "說服～（做）…" *undergo an operation* "接
受手術" 268. whose 用於人或非人均可。*look down* "俯視"
269. which 指前面整句。 270. which 具有形容詞作用。*which* advice ＝
and this advice。

（5）———————————————————————————————— 關係代名詞 **what**

271. I couldn't make out *what* my teacher was saying.

272. *What's* done cannot be undone.

273. *What* may be done at any time is done at no time.

274. *What* man has done, man can do.

275. I owe *what I am* to my mother.

276. I am not *what I was* ten years ago.

277. He spent *what money* he had on books.

278. She is *what is called* a talented woman.

279. John is very kind, and *what is better*, very wise.

280. Reading is to the mind *what* food is to the body.

【註】關係代名詞 what，本身兼做先行詞和關係代名詞，也可當形容詞。 271.～
274. what = that which；the thing(s) which 271. *make out* "了解"
273. *at any time* "隨時" 275.～276. cf. A man's worth lies not
so much in *what he has* as in *what he is*. （一個人的價值，不在於他
的財富，而在於他的品格。） 276. what I was "以前的我"

（5）———————————————————————— 關係代名詞**what**

271. 我不懂老師當時在講什麼。

272. 覆水難收。〔諺〕

273. 隨時可做的事，將沒有時間可做；拖延時日，終難實現。〔諺〕

274. 人已經做過的事，就能再做。

275. 我將今日的成就，歸功於我母親。

276. 我現在不是十年前的我了。

277. 他把他所有的錢都花在書本上了。

278. 她就是所謂有才能的女人。

279. 約翰非常仁慈，更好的是，非常聰明。

280. 閱讀對於心智，就好像食物對於人體的關係一樣。

---

277. what 當形容詞的用法＝He spent *all the money that* he had on books.　278.～280. 為what 的慣用語。　278. what is called＝what we call　279. *what is better* "更好的是" 相反詞為 *what is worse* "更糟的是"　280. A *is to* B *what* C *is to* D "A對於B就像C對於D 一樣"

（6）——————————————————— 關係代名詞 **as, but, than**

281. Give girls *the same* advantages *as* you give boys.

282. He is *as* nice a man *as ever lived*.

283. The story is written in *such* plain English *as* beginners can easily understand.

284. He comes from Tainan , *as* we can perceive from his accent.

285. *As is often the case with* students, he comes to school not to study, but to make friends and have fun.

286. There is *no one but* wants to live long.

287. His parents give him more money *than* is needed.

（7）——————————————————— 複合關係代名詞

288. You may give this ball to *whoever* wants it.

289. I am ready to do *whatever service* may be in my power.

290. You may read *whichever* you find interesting.

【註】281. ～ 285. as 和相關的片語一起使用。 281. the same ～ as … "和…同樣的～" 282. as ～ as … "和…一樣～" 284. as ＝which fact *come from ～* "從～來；～人" 285. 是慣用語。*as is often the case with～* "如常見於～的情形" *have fun* "玩樂" 286. ＝ There is no one that doesn't want to live long. 288. ～ 290. 複合關係代名

（6）————————————————————————關係代名詞 **as, but, than**

281. 把你給男孩們同樣的利益給女孩們。

282. 他是世上最好的人。

283. 這個故事是用初學者易懂的簡易英文寫的。

284. 他是台南人，我們可以從他的腔調中察覺到。

285. 就像學生常有的情形一樣，他來上學不是要學習，而是要交朋友和玩樂。

286. 沒有人不想長命百歲。

287. 他父母給他超過需要的錢。

（7）————————————————————————複合關係代名詞

288. 你可以把這個球給想要它的人。

289. 我願意盡力幫忙。

290. 你可以讀任何一本你覺得有趣的書。

詞 whoever = any one who, whatever = anything that, whichever = any one that　289. whatever 當形容詞。 ***be ready to*** ~ " 願意~ " ; 準備好~ " ***in one's power*** " 盡力 "

（8）———————————————— 關係副詞 where, when, why, how

291. The man came to live in *the small cave where* I used to spend most of my time in those days.

292. After you have done with the paper, put it back *where* it was.

293. Sooner or later *the day* will come *when* you will be thankful to your parents for it.

294. Can you tell me *how* I can get rid of her?

295. This is *how* I managed to escape the danger of being washed away.

296. There is no *reason why* I should not attend the meeting instead of my brother.

297. That is *why* I came home by way of Egypt.

（9）———————————————— 關係副詞 where, when 的補述用法

298. After walking a couple of hours, we came to *the lake, where* we put up for the night.

299. I visited *the city library, where* I happened to see an old friend of mine.

300. I am sorry I was late. *I was about to leave, when* the telephone rang.

【註】 291.～297. 關係副詞 where 表場所，when 表時間，why 表原因，how 表方法、狀態。為簡潔起見，關係副詞的先行詞常省略，如 292., 294., 295., 297. 即省略了先行詞。 292. *have done with* "做完" 293. *sooner or later* "遲早" *be thankful to ～ for …* "為了…感

（8）——————————————————— 關係副詞 where, when, why, how

291. 那人住進了那個小洞穴中，那些日子大部分時間我曾經在那洞中渡過。

292. 你看完報紙後，把它放回原來的地方。

293. 你因它而感謝你父母的一天，遲早會來到。

294. 你能不能告訴我怎樣才能擺脫她？

295. 這就是我如何設法而沒被沖走的方法。

296. 沒有理由說我不該代替我哥哥參加那會議。

297. 那就是爲什麼我經由埃及回家的原因。

（9）——————————————— 關係副詞 where, when 的補述用法

298. 走了兩個小時後，我們到了那湖，就在那兒過夜。

299. 我到市立圖書館去，在那裏我碰巧遇見了我的一位老朋友。

300. 對不起，我遲到了。我正要離開的時候，電話鈴響了。

謝〜” 294. *get rid of* “擺脫” 295. *manage to* “設法”
296. *instead of* “代替” 297. *by away of* “經由” 298. 〜 230.
where, when 的補述用法，在此 where ＝ and there；when ＝ and then
298. *put up* “住宿” 299. *happen to* “碰巧” 300. *be about to* “正
要”

10. Condition

（1）——————————————————— if, unless, provided, suppose, once

301. I will be much obliged *if* you will kindly let me have your answer now.

302. *Unless* we find other sources of energy, our way of life will change to a great extent.

303. I will agree to the proposal, *provided* you answer for the result.

304. *Suppose* Anne can't come, who will do the work?

305. *Once* you get into a bad habit, you will find it difficult to overcome.

（2）——————————————————— 祈使句＋ and（or）表條件

306. *Try to read the passage again and again*, *and* you cannot fail to get what the author means.

307. *Eat more*, *or* you will be hungry on the way.

308. *One more effort*, *and* you will succeed in the attempt.

309. *A few days more and* this fine theater will no longer exist.

310. *Talk of the devil and* he will appear.

【註】 301. ～ 305. 表條件的副詞子句中，連接詞以 if 為代表。其他 unless ＝ if～ not，provided（*or* providing）＝ if（only），suppose ＝ if，once ＝ if 301. *be obliged* "感激" 303. *agree to sth.* "同意某事" *answer for* "負責" 305. *get into* "養成（某習慣）"

10. 表條件的句型

301. 如果你現在告訴我你的答案，我會非常感激。

302. 除非我們發現其他的能源，否則我們的生活方式將作大幅度的改變。

303 如果後果你負責，我就同意這項提議。

304. 如果安不能來，誰將做這工作？

305 一旦你養成了壞習慣，你會發現很難克服它。

306. 試著一遍再一遍地去讀那段文章，你必定會了解作者的意思。

307. 多吃一點，不然你在路上會餓。

308. 再多努力一點，你的嘗試就會成功。

309. 再過幾天這座華麗的戲院就要消失了。

310. 說曹操曹操到。〔諺〕

306.～ 310. "祈使句＋ and, or" 可用 if 子句代換。例如： 308. ＝ If you make one more effort, you will succeed in the attempt. 306. *again and again* "一再地" *cannot fail to* "必定" 307. *on the way* "在途中"

（ 3 ）——————————— in case of, in case, on condition that, so long as

311. *In case of* rain, the garden party will be put off.

312. *In case* I am late, don't wait to start dinner.

313. Take your umbrella with you *in case* it rains.

314. You may use my car *on condition that* you drive it carefully.

315. *So long as* you are innocent, you need not fear anything.

316. I can read any book, *so long as* it is interesting.

（ 4 ）————————————————— 表條件的不定詞

317. *To tell you the truth*, Mr. Brown is heavily in debt.

318. *To speak frankly*, he is not a man to be relied upon.

319. *To do him justice*, he is not guilty of the crime.

320. *To hear Mary sing*, you would take her for a young girl.

【註】 311.～316. 其他表條件的片語中，*in case of*＋名詞 "如果"；*in case* （*that*）＋子句 "如果；以防萬一"；*on condition that* ＝ if；*so*〔*as*〕 *long as* ＝ if only "只要" 317. ～ 320. 爲不定詞表條件的用法。 317. ～ 319. 爲獨立不定詞片語，都有 "坦白說"的意思。

（3）——————————————— in case of, in case, on condition that, so long as

311. 如果下雨，園遊會就要延期。

312. 如果我遲到，別等我吃晚飯。

313. 帶著你的傘以防下雨。

314. 只要你小心駕駛，就可以用我的車子。

315. 只要你是無辜的，就不需要懼怕任何事。

316. 我能讀任何書，只要它有趣。

（4）————————————————————————— 表條件的不定詞

317. 告訴你實話，布朗先生負債累累。

318. 坦白說，他不是個可依賴的人。

319. 說句公道話，他並沒有犯罪。

320. 聽瑪麗唱歌，你會以爲她是個年輕的女孩。

---

317. *be in debt* "負債"　318. *rely upon* "依賴"　319. *to do him justice* "說句公道話"　*be guilty of* "犯～罪"　320. = If you hear Mary sing, …　*take ～ for* … "認爲～是…"

11. Concession

（ 1 ）——————— 表讓步的 though, although, (even)if, (even)though

321. Bill went to see the football game *though* his doctor had told him not to.

322 *Although* the restaurant was crowded, we managed to find a table.

323. *If* it is not all true, there is truth in what he says.

324. *Even if* it may cost me my life, I will do it to the last.

325. He will never be dishonest *even though* he should be reduced to poverty.

（ 2 ）———————————————————— 表讓步的 as, whether

326. *Tired as he was* after the game, Tom still prepared his lessons for two hours.

327. *Hero as he was*, he hesitated to run a risk.

328. *Clever though she may be*, she is not kind.

329. It doesn't matter *whether* you start now *or* tomorrow.

330. *Good or bad*, habits soon become a kind of second nature.

【註】 321. ～ 325. 用 though, although, (even) if, (even) though 表讓步，
有「即使～；雖然～」的意思的子句，就稱為讓步子句。

324. *to the last* "到最後為止" 326. ～ 330. 是 as, whether ～ or 在
讓步子句中的用法。 326. as = though，此句也可視為 As tired as he

11. 表讓步的句型

（1）──────────── 表讓步的 though, although, (even)if, (even)though

321. 雖然比爾的醫生告訴他不要去看橄欖球賽，他還是去了。

322. 儘管餐館很擁擠，我們設法找了一張桌子。

323. 雖然他的話不全是眞的，但也有些實情。
324. 卽使它可能使我喪失生命，我也要做到最後爲止。

325. 卽使他眞的淪爲貧困，也絕不會不誠實。

（2）──────────────── 表讓步的 as, whether

326. 雖然湯姆在比賽之後非常疲倦，他仍然準備了兩個小時的功課。

327. 他雖然是個英雄，但對於冒險的事也猶豫不決。
328. 雖然她很聰明，不過却不親切。
329. 你無論現在或是明天開始都沒關係。
330. 不論好的或壞的，習慣很快會變成一種第二天性。

---

was 的省略用法。　327. 以名詞起首的句型，注意名詞前不加冠詞。 *run a risk* “冒險” 329. whether A or B 在此是名詞子句，但有讓步的意味。 *second nature* “第二天性”

（ 3 ）————————————————————————— 表讓步的 -ever

331. *Whoever* may object, I will take part in the meeting.

332. *Whomever* you may ask, you'll get the same answer.

333. You can use *whosever* typewriter you like.

334. I am bound to go out *whatever* other people may say.

335. *Whichever* you choose, the others will be offended.

336. *Whichever* road you may take, it will bring you to the station.

337. *Whatever* business you may be engaged in, you can't hope for success without diligence.

338. *Wherever* you may hide it, the dog will find it.

339. *Whenever* I see these pictures, there comes back into my mind the memory of something I saw in Australia.

340. *However* much Tom may admire her, he is unlikely to ask her to be his wife.

【註】 331.～337. 是～ever 在讓步子句中的用法。 331. whoever 常當代名詞，為"不論誰"的意思。 *take part in* "參加" 334. *be bound to* "一定" 335. *be offended* "被觸怒" 336. 和 337. 的 whichever 和 whatever 當形容詞。 337. *be engaged in* "從事" 338. 和 339. 「wher-

（ 3 ）————————————————————— 表讓步的 **-ever**

331. 不論誰會反對，我都要參加那會議。

332. 你不論問誰，都會得到同樣的答案。

333. 任何人的打字機，只要你喜歡，都可以使用。

334. 不論其他人怎麼說，我都一定要出去。

335. 不論你選擇哪一個，都會觸怒別人。

336. 不論你走哪一條路，都能到車站。

337. 不論你從事什麼行業，不勤奮都無法成功。

338. 不管你把它藏在哪裏，這隻狗都會找到它。

339. 每當我看到這些照片，就會想起在澳洲所見的一些事物。

340. 不論湯姆多麼愛慕她，都不可能向她求婚。

---

ever 或 whenever ＋S＋V 」的形式表示 " 不論何處～或不論何時～ " 的意
味。　339. *come back into one's mind* " 回到某人的腦海 "
340.「 however ＋形容詞（副詞）＋S＋V 」的形式，同樣表示 " 不論～ "
的意思。　*be unlikely to* " 不可能 "

（4）──────────────────────────── 表讓步的 no matter ～

341. *No matter who* objects, I will support it.

342. I trust Betty *no matter what* people may say against her.

343. *No matter where* you may go, you must come back before dark.

344. *No matter how* you do it, the result is the same.

345. *No matter how often* he does it, he always makes a mistake.

（5）──────────────────── 表讓步的 in spite of, for (or with) all

346. *In spite of* frequent interruptions he completed the work in three days.

347. *For all* his poverty he was not ashamed of himself.

348. *With all* the means you can employ, you can't prevent it.

349. *Say what you will*, you won't be able to convince him.

350. *Be the weather ever so bad*, we must go to their rescue.

───────────────────────────────────────

【註】 341. ～ 345. 是 no matter ～ 在讓步子句中的用法。 341. no matter who = whoever "不論誰～" no matter 常和 what, where, when, how 等疑問詞連用。 345. *make a mistake* "犯錯" 346. ～ 350. 為其他表讓步的片語或子句。 346. 的 *in spite of* 347. 的 *for all* 和 348. *with all*

（4）——————————————————— 表讓步的 **no matter ～**

341. 不論誰反對，我都支持它。

342. 不論人們說貝蒂什麼壞話，我都信任她。

343. 不管你去哪裏，天黑以前必須回來。

344. 不管你怎麼做它，結果都是一樣的。

345. 不論他多麼常做它，總是會犯錯。

（5）——————————————— 表讓步的 **in spite of, for (or with) all**

346. 雖然常常中斷，他還是在三天內完成了那項工作。

347. 雖然他很貧窮，但並不自覺羞愧。

348. 儘管你用盡所有的方法，也無法阻止它。

349. 不論你怎麼說，也不能夠說服他。

350. 不管天氣多麼惡劣，我們都必須去救他們。

都是" 雖然；儘管 "的意思。　347. *be ashamed of* " 以～爲恥 "
349. 和 350. 爲表讓步的命令句。　349. = Whatever you may say, …
350. = However bad the weather may be, …　　*ever so* " 非常地 "

12. Object

（1）————————————————— so that ～, in order that ～的用法

351. I took my daughter to the hospital *so that* the doctor *might* give her a thorough examination.

352. I trod as lightly as possible *so（that）* the baby *might* not wake up.

353. She times the meal *so that* the hot rolls and meat *will* be at their best at the time.

354. The bridge is built wide *that* four cars *can* run side by side.

355. I raised my hand *in order that* a taxi *might* stop.

（2）————————————————————— 表目的的片語

356 Jack wishes to go to France *for the purpose of* studying art.

357. She went to America *with a view to* becoming a jazz singer.

358. I made the fence *for the sake of* safety.

359. He studied medicine *with the intention of* practicing.

360. I bought the tape recorder *for* learning foreign languages, not *for* listening to music.

【註】 that 子句為表目的的副詞子句，有「為了～」的意思。that 子句中用 may 比較正式，現在也有人用 can, could, will, would。 so that 的 that 可以省略。 352. *as ～ as possible* "盡可能～" *wake up* "醒來" 353. *at one's best* "處於最佳狀況" 354. *side by side* "並排著"

12. 表目的的句型

（1）―――――――――――― so that ～, in order that ～的用法

351. 我帶我女兒到醫院去，好讓醫師給她做徹底的檢查。

352. 我盡可能輕輕地走，以免吵醒嬰兒。

353. 她算好用餐時間，以使熱肉捲和肉到時候有最好的口味。

354. 這座橋建得很寬，四輛車子可以並排著行駛。

355. 我舉手以使計程車停下來。

（2）―――――――――――――――― 表目的的片語

356. 傑克希望到法國學藝術。

357. 她到美國爲了要成爲一個爵士歌手。

358. 我爲了安全起見，築了一道圍牆。

359. 他學醫爲了要掛牌行醫。

360. 我買這錄音機是爲了要學外語，不是要聽音樂。

---

356. ～ 360. 爲表目的的片語　356. *for the purpose of* ＋ V-ing
357. *with a view to* ＋V-ing　358. *for the sake of* ＋ N　359. *with
the intention of* ＋ V-ing　360. for " 爲了 "，也表目的。

（3）———————————— lest ～ should …, for fear （that）～ 的用法

361. Nancy turned away from her boyfriend *lest* he *should* see her tears.

362. He didn't tell his mother of the danger *for fear* she would be alarmed.

363. You should take care *for fear that* you *should* fall ill.

（4）———————————— 不定詞，in order to, so as to 的用法

364. My brother worked hard *to succeed*, but in vain.

365. Airplanes carry life vests *to enable* the passengers to use them in case of emergency.

366. He listened attentively *not to miss* a single word.

367. I stood aside for her *to enter*.

368. Tom started early *in order to get* to the appointed place before noon.

369. You should write slowly *in order not to make* mistakes.

370. He turned out the light *so as not to waste* electricity.

【註】361. lest he should see her tears = so that her boyfriend might not see her tears。*turn away from ～* "轉身背對～" 362. 363. *for fear （that）～* "以免～" 363. *take care* "小心" *fall ill* "生病" 364. ～ 370. to ～ 表目的，強調用法可用 *in order to ～*，*so as to ～* 其否

（3）——————————————— lest ～ should …, for fear（that）～ 的用法

361. 南西把臉轉過去背對她的男朋友，免得他看到她流淚。

362. 他沒把危險告訴他母親，以免她驚慌。

363. 你該小心點，以免生病了。

（4）——————————————— 不定詞，in order to, so as to 的用法

364. 我哥哥爲了要成功，努力地工作，但是無效。

365. 飛機上備有救生背心，使乘客在萬一緊急時能夠使用。

366. 他注意聽，不漏掉一個字。

367. 我站到一旁讓她進來。

368. 湯姆早早出發，以便能在中午以前到達指定地點。

369. 你應該慢慢寫，才不會出錯。

370. 他爲了不浪費電而把燈關掉。

定形爲 369. in order not to～　370. so as not to～　364. *in vain*
"無效"　365. *in case of* "萬一"　367. *stand aside* "站在一旁"
368. *get to* "到達"　370. *turn out* "關掉"

13. Result

(1)——————— so ～ that …, so that ～, such ～ that …, such that 的用法

371. Dick's income is *so* small *that* he can't afford to buy a car.

372. The Milky Way consists of *so* many stars *that* we can't count them.

373. He worked very hard at it, *so that* he has made great progress.

374. It was *such* a pleasant day *that* everyone was feeling cheerful.

375. Her loveliness was *such that* she seemed to everyone like a being from another world.

376. *Such* was his anxiety *that* he lost his health.

(2)——————————————— 表結果的「 to ＋名詞 」

377. *To my great astonishment*, nearly all the townspeople were dressed in rags.

378. Much *to the delight of the children*, the dog was on the point of doing some tricks.

379. He was *starved to death*.

380. Tom got angry and tore the letter *to pieces*.

【註】 371. 372. so ～（that）… 表結果。 372. *consist of* " 包括 " 373. so that 是 " 因此 " ， so ～ that … 是 " 如此～以致於… " 376. 可改成與 375. 相同的句型＝His anxiety was such that …　Such 放在句首時，主詞與動詞須倒裝。 377. ～ 380. to ＋名詞 表結果的用法 377. *to my great*

13. 表結果的句型

（1）———— so ~ that …, so that ~, such ~ that …, such that 的用法

371. 狄克的收入那麼少，所以買不起一輛車子。

372. 銀河包括的星球那麼多，所以我們無法數得清楚。

373. 他工作得非常努力，所以有了很大的進步。

374. 那是個非常愉快的日子，所以每個人都感到很快活。

375. 她是那麼美麗，對每個人來說她似乎就像是從另一個世界來的人。

376. 他是如此焦慮，以致於失去了健康。

（2）———————————————— 表結果的「 to ＋名詞」

377. 令我大感驚訝的是，幾乎所有的鎮民都衣衫襤褸。

378. 那隻狗正要要把戲，使得孩子們非常高興。

379. 他餓死了。
380. 湯姆很生氣，把信撕成碎片。

---

astonishment "令我大感驚訝的是" *be dressed in* "穿著"　378. *to the delight of sb.* "使某人高興的是"　*on the point of* ＋ V-ing " 正要 （做）~ "　380. *tear ~ to pieces* "把~撕成碎片"

（ 3 ）————————————————————————— 表結果的不定詞

381. I opened my eyes *to find* myself lying in a bed of a hospital.

382. My cousin came to the city *only to be disillusioned*.

383. Dick went to India *never to return*.

384. My grandfather lived *to be* over ninety.

（ 4 ）————————————————————————— too ～ to …的用法

385. My father was *too* drunk *to remember* to lock the back door.

386. He ran *too* quickly for me *to catch* up with.

387. He is *too* honest a man *to tell* a lie.

（ 5 ）————————————————————————— ～ enough to … , so ～ as to ～的用法

388. The man was not near *enough* for her *to distinguish* his features.

389. He was *so* careless *as to get* on the wrong train.

390. Her illness was *such as to cause* her sons great anxiety.

【註】 381. ～ 384. 不定詞表結果，可以用「連接詞＋S＋V」代替。 381. to find ＝ and I found 382. only to be ＝ but he was only to ～ 表對結果的失望。 383. never to return ＝ but he never returned 384. to be ＝ until he was 385. ～ 387. 為 too ～ to …的構句 385. ＝ My father was *so* drunk that he couldn*'t* remember ～ 386. *catch up*

(3) —————————————————————————— 表結果的不定詞

381. 我睜開眼睛，發現自己躺在醫院的床上。

382. 我表哥到城裏去，結果只感到幻滅。

383. 狄克去了印度，沒有再回來。

384. 我祖父活到九十多歲。

(4) —————————————————————————— too ~ to …的用法

385. 我父親喝了太多酒，以致於忘了鎖後門。

386. 他跑得太快，所以我趕不上。

387. 他太誠實了，所以不會說謊。

(5) —————————————————— ~ enough to …, so ~ as to ~的用法

388. 那人離她不夠近，以致於無法清楚認出他的容貌。

389. 他太不小心，以致於搭錯了火車。

390. 她病得那麼重，使得她的兒子們非常擔憂。

---

with "趕上" 387. 是「 too ＋形容詞＋a (or an)＋名詞」的句型 *tell a lie* "說謊" 388. ~ 390. ~ enough to …, so ~ as to …均為「非常~，以致於…」的意思。 389. = He was so careless that he got on the wrong train. *get on* "上（車）"

14. Cause & Reason

(1) ———————————————————————— 表原因、理由的 because

391. *Because* Mr. White is dressed in black, he looks like a priest.

392. We were delayed *because* there was heavy traffic on the highway.

393. He participated in the movement *not because* he wanted to, *but because* he was told to.

(2) ———————————————————————— 表原因、理由的 as, since

394. *As* my purse was stolen, I could not help feeling helpless.

395. *As* such is the case, he will not come here.

396. You need not go with me, *as* you are busy.

397. *Since* the work had tired him, he didn't begin his journey the next day.

(3) ———————————————————————— 表原因、理由的不定詞

398. She was surprised *to learn* that her mother had never been to the concert.

399. You are crazy *to let* Jane drive your car.

400. What a fool I was *not to find* a joke !

【註】 391. *look like* "看起來像" 392. heavy traffic "交通非常擁擠"
393. *not because ~ but because* … "不是因為～，而是因為…"
participate in "參加" 394. ~ 397. as, since 表原因、理由時，與
because 同義。 394. *cannot help* ＋ *V-ing* "不得不～" 396. 當 as 所表

14. 表原因、理由的句型

（1）────────────────────── 表原因、理由的 because

391. 由於懷特先生穿著黑色的衣服，所以看起來像個牧師。

392. 由於高速公路上交通非常擁擠，所以我們被耽誤了。

393. 他參加那運動並不是因為他要參加，而是因為別人要他參加。

（2）────────────────────── 表原因、理由的 as，since

394. 由於我的錢包被偷，我不禁感到絕望。
395. 由於情況如此，他將不會來這裏。
396. 你不必陪我去，因為你很忙。
397. 由於他工作得太疲倦了，因此第二天無法開始他的旅程。

（3）────────────────────── 表原因、理由的不定詞

398. 她很驚訝地知道她母親從來沒聽過音樂會。

399. 你讓珍開你的車子，眞是瘋了。
400. 我眞是個傻瓜，竟沒發現這是個笑話。

───────────────────────────────

示的原因已為對方所知時，其所引導的子句放在主要子句之後。　398.～400.
不定詞表原因、理由時，常和表感情的形容詞（glad, angry, surprised）連
用。　399. = You are crazy because you let ～

（4）──────────── that ～, now that ～, seeing that ～表原因、理由的用法

401. We are delighted *that* we have become friends again.

402. Is he crazy *that* he should do such a thing?

403. He gave up his task *not that* he disliked it, *but that* he was afraid he was unequal to it.

404. *Now that* you are here, I can go shopping.

405. You differ from him *in that* you are diligent in addition to your ability.

406. You may well be praised, *seeing that* you work so hard.

（5）──────────── 表原因、理由的 of ～, for ～, through ～

407. I am *glad of* the examination being over.

408. To my grief, my little brother *died of* influenza.

409. If you read *for* amusement alone, it is of little consequence how you read.

410. The baseball game was lost *through* his careless error.

────────────────────────────────

【註】 401.～403. that 表原因、理由時和 because 同義。 401. that we have 可改成 to have。 *become friends*（*again*）"言歸於好" 402. that he should do 可改成 to do。 403. *give up* "放棄" *be unequal to* "不能 勝任" 404.～406. *now*（*that*），*in that*，*seeing that* 等均表理由。 405. *differ from* ～ "與～不同" *in addition to* ～ "除了～外"

（4）──────────── that ～, now that ～, seeing that ～表原因、理由的用法

401. 我們很高興我們言歸於好了。
402. 他是不是瘋了，竟然做出這種事？
403. 他放棄他的工作並不是因為不喜歡它，而是因為怕無法勝任。

404. 既然你在這裏，我就可以去買東西。
405. 你與他不同，因為你除了有才能外，還很勤勉。

406. 你受嘉許是理所當然的，因為你工作非常努力。

（5）──────────── 表原因、理由的 of ～, for ～, through ～

407. 我很高興考試結束了。
408. 令我悲傷的是，我弟弟死於流行性感冒。
409. 如果你只是為了消遣而閱讀，那麼怎麼閱讀就不大重要了。

410. 由於他粗心大意的錯誤，這場棒球賽輸了。

---

406. *may well* ～ "很有理由～；大可～" 407.～410. 為表原因、理由
的片語。 407. *be glad of* "高興" 408. *die of* "死於" *to one's*
grief "令某人悲傷的是" 409. 和 410. 介系詞 for 和 through 均表理由。

（6）————————————————————— 表原因、理由的介系詞片語

411. The train was delayed *because of* heavy snow.

412. *Because of* the drought, the vegetables are scarce this year.

413. *Owing to* his frequent failures, he despaired of his success.

414. I can't accept your kind invitation *owing to* a previous engagement.

415. The airport was closed *on account of* the fog.

416. He was nervous *on account of* never having before spoken in public.

417. *For lack of* any better advice, I told him just to study harder.

418. Their business activities came to a standstill *for want of* money.

（7）———— what by ～ and what by …, what with ～ and what with … 的用法

419. *What by* coaxing and *what by* threatening, Mike carried out his plan.

420. *What with* the high prices, and *what with* the low wages, they found it difficult to get along.

【註】 411. ～ 418. 為表原因、理由的介系詞片語。 411. ～ 416. *because of ～*，*owing to ～*，*on account of ～* 都是 " 因為～ " 的意思。 413. *despair of ～* " 對～感絕望 " 416. *in public* " 公開地 " 417. 418. *for lack of ～*，*for want of ～* 都是 " 由於缺乏～ " 的意思。

（6）—————————————————————————— 表原因、理由的介系詞片語

411. 由於大雪，那班火車誤點了。

412. 由於乾旱，今年蔬菜很少。

413. 由於經常失敗，他對成功感到絕望。

414. 由於有約在前，我不能接受你好意的邀請。

415. 機場由於有霧而關閉。

416. 由於以前從沒公開講過話，所以很緊張。

417. 由於沒有更好的建議，我只告訴他更用功唸書。

418. 他們的業務活動由於缺錢而停頓。

（7）————— what by ～ and what by …, what with ～ and what with…的用法

419. 半哄騙半威脅，邁克實現了他的計畫。

420. 一方面因為物價高，一方面因為薪水低，他們發覺很難過日子。

---

419. 420. *what by～ and what by …, what with ～ and what with …*
都是 " 一方面由於～，一方面由於… " 的意思。　419. *carry out* " 實現 "
420. *get along* " 過活 "

15. Time

(1) ───────────────────────────────── **when** 子句的用法

421. The train had started *when* I got to the station.
422. The boy wants to become a scientist *when* he grows up.
423. It's foolish to take a taxi *when* you can easily walk to the station.

(2) ───────────────────────────────── **as** 子句的用法

424. *As* I called for Kate at three, she had not dressed herself as yet.
425. He showed his pictures *as* we walked along.
426. *As* years went on, she was liable to fall ill.

(3) ───────────────────────────────── **while , after** 子句的用法

427. John slipped out of the room *while* we were engaged in a hot discussion.
428. Strike the iron *while* it is hot.
429. Make hay *while* the sun shines.
430. There was nothing left *after* he had finished his dinner.

───

【註】 421.～ 423. when 子句的用法。 when "當時" 421. *get to* "到達"
424.～ 426. 為 as 子句的用法。 as 與 when 意思相同。 424. *call for*
"接（某人）" *as yet* "至（當時）為止" 426. *go on* "（時間）過

15. 表時間的句型

(1) ———————————————————————— when 子句的用法

421. 當我到達車站時，火車已經開了。

422. 這男孩長大後想要做科學家。

423. 當你可以輕易地走到車站，却搭計程車，這樣是愚笨的。

(2) ———————————————————————— as 子句的用法

424. 當我三點鐘去接凱特時，她還沒有穿好衣服呢。

425. 我們走路的時候，他拿出他的照片給我們看。

426. 隨著年歲的增加，她很容易生病。

(3) ———————————————————————— while , after 子句的用法

427. 當我們正在熱烈討論時，約翰溜出了房間。

428. 打鐵趁熱。〔諺〕

429. 有太陽時快晒草；把握時機。〔諺〕

430. 他吃完晚飯後，什麼都沒剩下了。

去" *be liable to* "易於～的"　　427.～430. while , after 子句的用
法。　while 有 during～的意思。　　427. *slip out of* "溜出"
be engaged in "從事於"。

(4) —————————————————— **before** 子句的用法

431. My cousin waited a long time *before* the plane arrived at the airport.

432. Look *before* you leap.

433. Don't count your chickens *before* they are hatched.

434. I had *not* walked a mile *before* I got tired.

435. It was *long before* he got familiar with French.

436. It will *not* be *long before* his son supports his family.

(5) —————————————————— **till , once , since** 子句的用法

437. I had to wait there *till* the sky cleared up.

438. *Once* you have made a promise, you must keep it.

439. *It is* seventeen years *since* I gave up teaching and started to live an independent life of the pen.

440. I haven't heard from you *since* you went to live in London.

【註】 431. ～ 436. 為 before 子句的用法。 before "～以前" 435. *get familiar with* "精通" 437. ～ 440. 為 till , once, since 子句的用法。 till ～ "到～ 為止" once "一旦" 439. =Seventeen years have passed since ～.

（4）———————————————————— before 子句的用法

431. 飛機到達機場以前，我表哥等了很久。

432. 三思而行。〔諺〕

433. 不要打如意算盤；不要過早樂觀；小鷄孵出後才算數。〔諺〕

434. 我還走不到一哩路就累了。

435. 他熟悉法文花了好長一段時間。

436. 過不久他兒子就會維持他的家庭了。

（5）———————————————————— till, once, since 子句的用法

437. 我必須在那裏等到天氣放晴。

438. 一旦你許下一個承諾，你就必須遵守。

439. 自從我放棄敎書，開始過著寫作的獨立生活，已有十七年了。

440. 自從你到倫敦居住後，我就沒有聽到你的消息。

---

437. *clear up* "放晴"　438. *make a promise* "許下承諾"
439. *give up*＋*V-ing* "放棄～"　440.「S＋現在完成式＋since ～」
"聽到～的消息"

(6) ─────────────────────────────── until 子句的用法

441. *It was not until* Jack warned me *that* I became aware of the danger.

442. All the while a certain habit is forming and hardening, *until* at last we find ourselves helpless.

(7) **as soon as~, no sooner~than…, hardly~when…, scarcely~when…** 的用法

443. *As soon as* he caught sight of me, he avoided me.

444. *No sooner* had he finished it *than* he went out.

445. *Hardly* had he received the letter *when* (*or before*) he started for Paris.

446. *Scarcely* had he been out of sight *when* (*or before*) she entered the door.

(8) ──────────── **the moment, the instant, every time, by the time** 的用法

447. I knew who it was *the moment* he spoke.

448. *The instant* he saw me he jumped off his horse.

449. *Every time* I see this picture, it reminds me of those happy days.

450. *By the time* you are dressed, breakfast will be ready.

【註】 441. 442.爲 until 子句的用法。until 和 till 同義。　441. *It was not until~that…* " 直到~才… "　*become aware of* " 察覺 "　422. *all the while* " 自始至終 "　443.~446. *as soon as~, no sooner~than…*, *hardly* (*or scarcely*)…*when* (*or before*)~均爲 " 一~就… "。　注意 no sooner, hardly, scarcely 等否定字放句首時，主詞和助動詞要倒裝。

（6）——————————————————————— until 子句的用法

441. 直到傑克警告我，我才察覺到危險。

442. 自始至終某個習慣養成了，固定了，一直到最後我們發現沒有辦法改變了。

（7）——————————— as soon as～, no sooner～than…, hardly～
when…, scarcely ～when …的用法

443. 他一看見我就躲開我。

444. 他一完成它就出去了。

445. 他一接到信就動身到巴黎。

446. 她一進門，他就不見了。

（8）——————— the moment, the instant, every time, by the time 的用法

447. 他一說話，我就知道是誰了。

448. 他一看到我，就從馬上跳下來。

449. 每次我一看到這張照片，就使我想起那些快樂的日子。

450. 你一穿好衣服，早餐就會準備好。

---

443. *catch sight of* "看見"　445. *start for* "動身前往"　446. *be out of sight* "看不見"　447.448. *the moment* ～和 *the instant* ～"一～就"　449. every time ＝whenever　*remind ～of* … "使～想起…"　450. *by the time* "在～之時"

（9）————————————————————————— 表時間的介詞片語

451. *During my stay* in France, I came to love the man.

452. She danced for joy *at the news*.

453. She could not help being a little frightened *at the thought of* her husband taking such a long journey.

454. That evening we reached home *at the stroke of* six.

455. He hit on this idea *at the age of* fifteen.

456. She fainted *at the sight of* blood pouring from her son's body.

457. *On arrival* in this town, he was surprised to find a lot of Chinese restaurants.

（10）————————————————————————— 表時間的動名詞片語

458. *After finishing* his task, he watched the baseball game on television.

459. Take great care *in crossing* the busy street.

460. *On glancing* at this letter I concluded it to be that of which I was in search.

【註】451.～457. 爲介系詞（片語）表時間的用法。　451. during my stay＝while I was staying　452. at the news＝when she heard the news　*dance for joy*"因高興而舞蹈"　453. at the thought of＝when she thought of　*cannot help＋V-ing*"不由得～"　454. at the stroke of＝when it struck　455. at the age of fifteen＝when he was fifteen years old

（9）──────────────── 表時間的介詞片語

451. 在我留法期間，我愛上了那個人。
452. 當她聽到那消息時，她高興得跳起來。
453. 她一想到她丈夫正在長途旅行，不由得有些驚恐起來。

454. 那晚我們在鐘敲六點時到家。
455. 他在十五歲時想到了這個主意。
456. 她一看到血從她兒子身上流出來，就昏倒了。

457. 一到達這個城鎮，他很驚訝地發現很多中國餐館。

（10）──────────────── 表時間的動名詞片語

458. 他做完了工作以後，就看電視棒球賽。

459. 越過繁忙的街道時，要非常小心。
460. 我一看到這封信，就斷定它是我在找的那封。

---

hit on "忽然想到"　456. at the sight of ＝when she saw　457. on arrival＝when he arrived　458.～460.「介系詞＋動名詞」常表時間。　458. after finishing＝after he finished　459. in crossing ＝when you cross　*take great care* "非常小心"　460. on glancing＝as soon as I glanced　*conclude～to be…* "對～下…結論"　*be in search of* "尋找"

16. Manner & Others

(1) ────────────────────────────── 表狀態的 **as**

461. He did his work **as** his teacher instructed.
462. PTA, **as** you all know, stands for Parent-Teacher Association.
463. His report, **as** I remember, was highly esteemed.

(2) ────────────────────────── **as it is, as they are** 的用法

464. Don't touch my book. Leave it **as it is**.
465. We ought to try to see things **as they are**.
466. If I had enough time, I could go there. **As it is**, I can go nowhere.

(3) ────────────────────────── **as if** (*or* **though**) 的用法

467. Bob speaks **as if** he knew everything.
468. She talked **as though** she had seen it with her own eyes.

(4) ────────────────────────── **as~, so** …的用法

469. **As** food is to the body, **so** is reading to the mind.
470. **As** a man sows, **so** shall he reap.

───────────────────────────────────────

【註】461.～463. as＝in the way that 的意思，引導副詞子句表狀態。　463.的as 表限定，作＂就～＂解。　464.465.as it is 放在句尾，作＂照原來的樣子＂解。 466.As it is 放在句首時，作＂事實上＂解。　467.和468. **as if** (*or* **though**)

16. 表狀態和其他的句型

(1)─────────────────────────────── 表狀態的 **as**

461. 他照他老師的指定做作業。
462. 如大家所知，PTA代表母姊會。

463. 就我所記得的，他的報告獲得很高的評價。

(2)─────────────────────── **as it is , as they are** 的用法

464. 別碰我的書，就讓它保持原來的樣子。
465. 我們應該試著去了解事情的現況。
466. 如果我有足夠的時間，我就能去那裏。事實上，我哪裏也不能去。

(3)─────────────────────── **as if**（ *or* **though**）的用法

467. 鮑伯說話的樣子，就好像他知道每一件事一樣。
468. 她說話的樣子，就好像她親眼看過它似的。

(4)─────────────────────── **as ～ , so** …的用法

469. 閱讀之於心智，猶如食物之於身體。
470. 要怎麼收穫先怎麼栽；種瓜得瓜。〔諺〕

引導假設法的子句，作 " 好像 " 解。　469.和470. *as～so* … " …猶如～一樣 "
as 是連接詞，引導副詞子句修飾後面的相關副詞 **so**。　469. ＝Reading is to
the mind what food is to the body.（ cf. 280.）

(5) ——————————— as (or so) long as , as (or so) far as 的用法

471. It matters little who finds the truth, *so long as* the truth is found.

472. You'll have to look after her *as long as* you live.

473. *So far as* I know, nothing like that has ever happened before.

474. *As far as* I'm concerned, I have no objection to the plan.

475. *As far as* the eye can reach, nothing can be seen but water.

(6) ——————————— like , as for , as regards 的用法

476. The cat darted out of the room *like* lightning.

477. *As for* me, I have nothing to do with the matter.

478. *As regards* my daughter's future, I'll think about it later.

(7) ——————————— 表附帶狀態 with

479. He thought the matter over *with his eyes closed*.

480. I saw a girl standing at the gate *with tears in her eyes*.

【註】471. 472. *as (or so) long as* "只要"，引導副詞子句，表條件。　473.~
475. *as (or so) far as* "就～所"。　476. like "像～"，是介系詞。
477. 478. *as for* 和 *as regards* 都是"關於～"的意思，整個片語視爲介詞，

（5）──────────── as（or so）long as, as（or so）far as 的用法

471. 事實是誰發現的沒關係，只要被發現就好了。

472. 只要你活著，你就必須照顧她。

473. 就我所知，以前沒有過這樣的事情發生。

474. 至於我，我不反對這個計畫。

475. 就眼睛所能看見的，除了水以外，看不到任何東西。

（6）──────────── like, as for, as regards 的用法

476. 那隻貓像閃電一樣，從房間裏竄出來。

477. 至於我，我和這件事情無關。

478. 關於我女兒的未來，稍後我要好好想一想。

（7）──────────── 表附帶狀態的 with

479. 他閉著眼睛考慮這件事情。

480. 我看見一個女孩站在門口，眼裏含著淚水。

────────────────────────────────

稱片語介詞。（詳見文法寶典 p.544）　477. *have nothing to do with*～
"與～無關"　479. 480.「with＋受詞＋p.p. 或形容詞…」為表附帶狀態
ㄉ分詞。　479. *think over* "考慮"

17. Comparison

（1）—————————————————————— as ＋原級＋ as

481. Your advice was *as* helpful *as* my uncle's.

482. He is *not as*（*or so*）rich *as* he used to be.

483. *Nothing* in the world was *as* impractical *as* his plan.

484. You must speak English *as* often *as* *possible* if you want to improve your English.

（2）—————————————————————— as ～ as 表倍數的用法

485. Kate has three times *as* many disks *as* I.

486. The population of Rome is twice *as* large *as* that of this city.

（3）—————————————————————— as ～ as 的慣用語

487. Shakespeare is *as* great a dramatist *as* ever lived in England.

488. Taipei is *as* large *as any* city in Taiwan.

489. He remained *as* silent *as ever* during the lesson.

490. It is difficult for me to read *as* many *as* ten pages of this difficult English book.

──

【註】 481. as ＋原級＋ as 是原級比較。　482. 483. 否定句時，第一個 as 可改為 so。*not as*（*or so*）～ *as* … "不像…那樣～"　483. *in the world* ＝ *at all*　485. 486. ～倍數＋ as ＋形容詞或副詞＋ as … "～是…的幾倍"

17. 表比較的句型

（1）———————————————————— as ＋原級＋ as

481. 你的忠告和我叔叔的一樣有用。
482. 他不像過去那麼有錢。
483. 世上再也沒有事情像他的計畫一樣地不實用。
484. 如果你要改進你的英文，就必須盡可能地常說它。

（2）———————————————— as ～ as 表倍數的用法

485. 凱特的唱片是我的三倍多。
486. 羅馬的人口是這個城市人口的兩倍。

（3）———————————————— as ～ as 的慣用語

487. 莎士比亞是英國有史以來最偉大的劇作家。

488. 台北是台灣最大的都市。
489. 他在那堂課上保持著前所未有的沉默。
490. 這麼難的英文書，即使是讀十頁，對我來說也是困難的。

487.～489. 爲用原級表最高級。其他例如：He is as poor as a church mouse.（他像教堂老鼠一樣窮。）　487. 第二個 as 是關係代名詞，引導形容詞子句修飾 dramatist。　490. *as many as* ～ "和～一樣多"

（4）――――――――――――――――――――――――――――― 原級比較的慣用語

491. A man's worth lies *not so much* in what he has *as* in what he is.

492. Betty did*n't so much as* take a glance at the newspaper.

493. He went out *without so much as* saying good-bye.

494. I waited there for twenty minutes――they seemed *as many* hours to me.

495. You *might as well* throw your money away *as* lend it to him.

（5）――――――――――――――――――――――――――――― 比較級的基本句型

496. I like Taipei *better than any other* city in Taiwan.

497. *Which* do you think is *more difficult*, mathematics *or* physics ?

498. The pen is *mightier than* the sword.

499. I never saw a *finer* sight *than* the figure of Mt. Ali against the blue.

500. The hotels report *fewer* travelers this summer *than* last.

【註】 491. *not so much ~ as* … "與其說~，倒不如…" 492. *not so much as* ＋V "甚至不~" *take a glance at* ~ "對~一瞥" 493. *without so much as* ＋V-ing "連~也不" 494. *as many* "一樣多的"

（4）————————————————————————————— 原級比較的慣用語

491. 一個人的價值，不在於他的財富，而在於他的品格。

492. 貝蒂對報紙甚至連瞥也不瞥一眼。

493. 他甚至連再見也沒說，就出去了。

494. 我在那裏等了二十分鐘——這二十分鐘對我來說，就像二十個小時一樣。

495. 與其把錢借給他，倒不如扔掉。

（5）————————————————————————————— 比較級的基本句型

496. 台灣的都市中，我對台北的喜歡勝過其他都市。

497. 你認為數學和物理學，哪一個比較難？

498. 文勝於武；筆誅勝於劍伐。〔諺〕

499. 我從沒看過比在藍天襯托下的阿里山形象更美的景色了。

500. 旅館公布，今年夏天的觀光客比去年少。

---

495. *might as well* ＋V～*as* … "與其…還不如～" 　498.類似的諺語有：
The tongue is not steel, yet it cuts. (舌雖非鋼，但能傷人。) 　499. *a-
gainst the blue* "藍天襯托下" 　500.為「比較級＋名詞＋than～」的形式。

（6）────────────────────────── 應注意的比較級

501. The director came to office at nine this morning *later than* usual.

502. *The latter* speaker was not so eloquent as *the former*.

503. She is more intelligent, but *less beautiful than* Mary.

504. This one is *the better of the two* compositions.

505. He is *more wise than diligent*.

506. Some girls *would rather* be single *than* get married.

（7）────────────────────────── 比較級的慣用語（a）

507. I *can't* put up with his idleness *any longer*.

508. *The older* I grew, *the more* convinced I became of the folly of the public.

509. There is continually *more and more* to read and *less and less* time for reading.

510. Everyone was *more or less* interested in the arts.

─────────────────────────────

【註】501. later 指 " 時間較遲 "　　502. latter 指 " 順序較後者 "　　503.「less＋原級＋ than ～」指 " 比～不 "　　504.「the ＋比較級＋ of the two 」指 " 二者之中較～的一個 "　　505. 同一人的兩種性質的比較，用「more ＋原級＋ than ＋原級」　　506. *would rather ～ than* ＋原形 V " 寧可～也不… "

（6）――――――――――――――――――――――――――――――――應注意的比較級

501. 董事長今天早上九點才到辦公室，比平常晚。

502. 後一位演講者沒有前一位來得流利。

503. 她比較聰明，不過沒有瑪麗漂亮。

504. 這篇是這兩篇作文中較好的一篇。

505. 與其說他勤勉，不如說聰明。

506. 有些女孩寧可單身，也不結婚。

（7）――――――――――――――――――――――――――――――比較級的慣用語（a）

507. 我再也忍受不了他的懶惰。

508. 我長得越大，就越確信大衆的愚昧。

509. 不斷地有越來越多的書要讀，讀書的時間却越來越少。

510. 每個人都或多或少對藝術有興趣。

---

get married “結婚”　507. *put up with* “忍受”　508.「the＋比較級～，the＋比較級…」“越～，就越…” *become convinced of* “確信”　509.「比較級＋and＋比較級」“越來越～”

(8)—————————————————————————————————— 比較級的慣用語（b）

511. I know he has worked well, but *none the less* I must punish him on this occasion.

512. His father suddenly passed away, and *what was worse*, his mother was taken ill.

513. I like the girl *all the better* for her cleverness.

514. Learning makes a man wise, but a fool is made *all the more foolish* by it.

515. I do not even suggest that he is negligent, *still less* (*or much less*) that he is dishonest.

516. Everyone has a right to his property, *much more* (*or still more*) to his life.

517. He has *no more than* a thousand dollars with him.

518. I was *not more than* two blocks when I came across a friend of mine.

519. There were *no less than* twelve canaries in the cage.

520. I paid *not less than* twenty dollars for this bag.

【註】 511. *none the less* "仍然" *on this occasion* "這次"　512. *What is worse* "更糟的是"　*pass away* "去世"　*be taken ill* "生病" 513. all the better for～ "爲了～而更"　515. 516. much less (*or* still less)"更不用說"是否定意味，much more (*or* much less)是肯定意味。

（8）――――――――――――――――――――――――――― 比較級的慣用語（**b**）

511. 我知道他工作表現很好，不過這次我還是必須處罰他。

512. 他的父親突然去世，更糟的是，他的母親生病了。

513. 由於她的聰明，使我更喜歡她。

514. 學識使得一個人變聰明，不過一個愚笨的人也會因它而變得更笨。

515. 我甚至連他的疏忽都沒說出，更不用說他的不誠實了。

516. 每個人對他的財產都有權利，更不用說生命了。

517. 他身上只有一千塊錢。

518. 我在不超過兩條街的地方，偶然遇到我的朋友。

519. 在那籠裏的金絲雀多達十二隻。

520. 這個袋子我付了至少二十元。

---

517. *no more than* = only "只"　518. *not more than* "不超過"
come across "偶然遇到"　519. *no less than* = as many (*or* much)
as "多達"　520. *not less than* = at least "最少"

（9）──────────── no more ～ than …和 no less ～ than …的用法

521. I am *no more* concerned in the crime *than* you are.

522. Mary did *not* know of chamber music *any more than* she did of jazz.

523. A whale is *no less* a mammal *than* a horse is.

524. She is *no less* beautiful *than* her sister.

525. Light is *not less* necessary *than* fresh air to health.

（10）──────────── senior , junior , superior , prefer 的用法

526. Frank is *senior to* my brother by two years.

527. He is three years *junior to* me, but excels me in knowledge and wisdom.

528. She is *superior to* me in speaking English.

529. I *prefer* to stand *rather than* (*to*) sit.

530. I *prefer* reading books *to* watching television.

【註】521. 522. no more ～ than … = not ～ any more than … "和……一樣不～"
be concerned in ～ "與～有關連"　523. no less ～ than … "和……一樣～"
525. not less ～ than … "也許比…更～"　526. *be senior to* ～ "比～年

（9）──────────── no more～than … 和 no less ～ than …的用法

521. 我和你一樣，與這件犯罪案沒關連。

522. 瑪麗對室內樂和爵士樂同樣不懂。

523. 鯨魚跟馬同樣是哺乳動物。

524. 她與她姊姊同樣漂亮。

525. 光線和新鮮空氣一樣，對健康都是必須的。

（10）──────────── senior , junior , superior , prefer 的用法

526. 法蘭克比我弟弟大兩歲。

527. 他比我小三歲，不過知識和智慧却勝過我。

528. 她英文說得比我好。

529. 我寧可站著也不願坐著。

530. 我比較喜歡讀書而較不喜歡看電視。

長 ” 　527. *be junior to* ～ “ 比～年小 ” 　528. *be superior to* ～ “ 比～
好 ” 　529. *prefer to* ＋原形 V ＋*rather than* ＋原形 V “寧可～也不願…”
＝ 530. *prefer* ＋ V-ing ＋ *to* ＋ V-ing（詳見文法寶典 p. 204 ）

531. ***The most dangerous*** thing is to try to appear what you are not.

532. This is ***the most exciting story*** that I have ever heard.

533. This question is ***the least difficult*** of all.

534. She is ***by far the most talented*** pianist in the world.

535. I feel ***happiest*** when I read alone in my own room.

536. California is ***the third largest state*** in the United States.

537. This is my ***best dress*** and that is my ***second best***.

538. ***The most careful*** observation would not have revealed the mystery.

539. ***Most people*** I have met believe they are paid much less than they deserve.

540. We found that she was ***a most charming*** young lady.

【 註 】 533. *the least difficult* " 最容易的 "　　534. by far the ＋最高級形容詞
" 最～的 "（ 詳見文法寶典 p. 207 ）　　535. 絕對最高級之前不加 the （詳見文
法寶典 p. 205 ） cf. The lake is *deepest at this point*.(這湖在這裏最深。)

（11）──────────────────────── 最高級的用法

531. 想試著表現出不是眞正的你，是最危險的事。

532. 這是我所聽過最動人的故事。

533. 這個問題是所有問題中，最容易的一個。

534. 她是世界上最有才能的鋼琴家。

535. 當我一個人在自已房間讀書的時候，感到最快樂。

536. 加州是美國第三大州。

537. 這件是我最好的衣服，那件是第二好的。

538. 最審愼的觀察也揭露不了那個謎。

539. 大部分我認識的人以爲，他們得到的報酬比他們應得的少多了。

540. 我們發現她是個非常迷人的年輕淑女。

The lake is *the deepest* in Taiwan.（這湖是台灣最深的。） 536. 537. 在最高級前加序數，表「第～」的意思。　538. 此最高級含有 even 的意思。
539. 的 most 是 " 大部分 "　540. most = very

（12）——————————————————————— 最高級的慣用語

541. Mr. Chen was ***the last*** person I had expected to see.

542. I sent him a nice present, but he was ***not in the least*** pleased with it.

543. She will be in hospital for ***at least*** ten days.

544. My parents give me an allowance of ***at most*** three thousand dollars a month.

545. His play would be ***at best*** a second-rate melodrama.

546. I have to ***make the best of*** the small room.

547. We should ***make the most of*** our opportunity.

（13）——————————————————————— 與最高級相同意義的用法

548. In his class Ted was ***second to none*** in French.

549. It was ***next to impossible*** to swim across this large river.

550. The Taiwan countryside in October is beautiful ***beyond description***.

【註】541. *the last* ＋N "最不願～的…"　542. *not in the least* "一點也不"
be pleased with ～ "喜歡～"　543. *at least* "至少"　544. *at most*
"最多"　545. *at best* "充其量"　second-rate "二流的；劣等的"

（12）─────────────────────────最高級的慣用語

541. 陳先生是我最不希望看到的人。

542. 我送他一份精美的禮物，不過他一點也不喜歡。

543. 她至少要住院十天。

544. 我父母一個月最多給我三千塊零用錢。

545. 他的戲劇充其量只不過是個第二流的鬧劇。

546. 我必須充分利用這個小房間。

547. 我們必須儘量利用我們的機會。

（13）─────────────────────與最高級相同意義的用法

548. 泰德的法文在他班上不亞於任何人。

549. 要游過這條大河幾乎不可能。

550. 台灣十月的鄉間美得無法形容。

---

546. *make the best of* "充分利用" 　547. *make the most of* "善加利用" 　548. *second to none* "不亞於任何人" 　549. *next to impossible* "幾乎不可能" 　550. *beyond description* "無法形容"

18. Ellipsis

（1）──────────────────────── 諺語的省略用法

551. No pains, no gains.

552. Out of sight, out of mind.

553. Spare the rod and spoil the child.

554. The sooner, the better.

555. Better bend than break.

556. Easy come, easy go.

557. When in Rome, do as the Romans do.

558. First come, first served.

（2）──────────────────────── 告示的省略用法

559. Wet paint.

560. No visitors allowed while at work.

【註】 551. (*If one takes*) no pains, (*one will have*) no gains. 552. *out of mind* "遺忘" (*If a man is*) out of sight, (*he will go*) out of mind. *out of sight* "看不到" 553. Spare the rod and (*you will*) spoil the child. 554. The sooner (*you do it*), the better (*it will be*). 555. (*It is*) better (*to*) bend than (*to*) break.

18. 省略句

（1）────────────────────────────── 諺語的省略用法

551. 不勞則無獲；吃得苦中苦，方為人上人。〔諺〕

552. 離久則情疏；眼不見，心不念。〔諺〕

553. 不打不成器。〔諺〕

554. 愈快愈好。〔諺〕

555. 寧屈不斷；大丈夫能屈能伸。〔諺〕

556. 來得容易，去得快。〔諺〕

557. 入境隨俗。〔諺〕

558. 先到先得；捷足先登。〔諺〕

（2）────────────────────────────── 告示的省略用法

559. 油漆未乾。

560. 工作時間謝絕訪客。

---

556. (*If they*) easy come, (*they will*) easy go.　557. When
(*you are*) in Rome, do as the Romans do.　558. (*If you*)
first come, (*you will be*) first served.　559. (*Beware of the*)
wet paint. ***beware of*** "注意；小心"　560. No visitors (*are*) allowed
while (*they are*) at work. ***at work*** "工作中"

（3）——————————————————————「S＋V」的省略

561. Though old, my aunt is not slow of understanding.

562. While reading, I fell asleep.

563. He never speaks unless spoken to.

564. This work is not as easy as you think.

565. " Will he come soon？" " I'm afraid not."

566. Better have nothing to do with the matter.

567. What a pity he passed away so young！

（4）——————————————————————— 不定詞的省略

568. You don't have to be concerned with the project if you don't want to.

569. I am very sorry if I hurt your feelings. I didn't mean to.

570. He went on, but I didn't care to.

【註】561. Though (*she is*) old, … *be slow of* "～遲鈍" 562. While (*I was*) reading,… *fall asleep* "睡著" 563. …unless (*he is*) spoken to 564. …as you think (*it is*). 565. I'm afraid (*he will*) not (*come soon*). 566. 常用於口語中。(*You had*) better have nothing… *have nothing to do with* ～ "和～無關" 567. What a pity (*it is*

（3）──────────────────────────「S＋V」的省略

561. 我嬸嬸雖然老了，不過理解力並不遲鈍。

562. 我在讀書的時候睡著了。

563. 除非別人找他講話，否則他從不說話。

564. 這件工作不像你想得那麼容易。

565. 「他會很快來嗎？」「恐怕不會。」

566. 最好別和那件事扯上關係。

567. 他那麼年輕就死，多可惜啊！

（4）──────────────────────── 不定詞的省略

568. 如果你不想的話，不必參與這項計畫。

569. 如果我傷了你的感情，非常抱歉。我並不是有意的。

570. 他繼續前進，但是我並不想這樣。

---

that) he passed away … ***pass away*** "死" 568. … if you don't want to (*be concerned with the project*). ***be concerned with*** "參與" 569. … I didn't mean to (*hurt your feelings*). 570. … I didn't care to (*go on*). ***care to*** ～ "想～；要～"

(5) ─────────────────────────────── 會話中的省略

571. Just a moment, please.

572. Doesn't matter.

573. See you tomorrow.

574. Good luck to you.

(6) ─────────────────────────────── 名詞的省略

575. To know is one thing, and to practice quite another.

576. We spent a week at my uncle's.

577. Correct errors if any.

(7) ─────────────────────────────── 其他的省略

578. Mr. Brown is rich, but his uncle is five times as rich.

579. I have lost my watch and my brother his bag.

580. She believed in me when no one else would.

───

【註】 571. (*Wait*) just a moment, please.   572. (*It*) doesn't matter.
573. (*I'll*) see you tomorrow.   574. (*I wish*) good luck to you.
575. …, and to practice (*is*) quite another (*thing*).   576. …at

(5) ──────────────────────────────── 會話中的省略

571. 請等一下。

572. 沒關係。

573. 明天見。

574. 祝好運。

(6) ──────────────────────────────── 名詞的省略

575. 知道是一回事，做又是一回事。

576. 我們在我叔叔家渡過了一個星期。

577. 如果有錯，請更正。

(7) ──────────────────────────────── 其他的省略

578. 布朗先生很有錢，不過他的叔叔比他富有五倍。

579. 我丟了手錶，我哥哥丟了袋子。

580. 當沒有其他人信任我時，她信任我。

---

my uncle's (*house*).　577. ···if (*there are*) any (*errors*).　578. ···
five times as rich (*as he*).　579. ···and my brother (*has lost*) his
bag.　580. ···no one else would (*believe in me*). *believe in* "信任"

19. Parenthesis

（1）────────────────────────────── 字的插入

581. Finally, *however*, Mr. Harris got used to living in that city.

582. It is necessary, *therefore*, that I should take over the office in place of my father.

583. He was *indeed* badly in need of money.

（2）────────────────────────── 用片語的插入譯成英文

584. I seldom, *if ever*, go to church.

585. There is little, *if any*, difference between their manners and customs.

586. You mustn't, *by the way*, eat bread with knife and fork.

587. The success is, *after all*, due to his effort.

588. I found, *to my great surprise*, that he was still alive.

589. She is old, *to be sure*, but she is healthy.

590. My teacher is, *so to speak*, a walking dictionary.

───

【註】 581.～583. 是單字的插入。 584.～590. 是片語的插入。 581. *get used to* "習慣於" 582. *take over* "接管" *in place of* "代替" 583. *be in need of* "需要" 584. (*seldom*) *if ever* "難得地" 585. *few* (*little*) *if any* "即使有，也很少" manners and customs

19. 插 入 語

（1）──────────────────────────── 字的插入

581. 無論如何，最後哈利斯先生習慣了住在那個城市。

582. 因此，我代替我父親接管職務是必須的。

583. 他確實非常需要錢。

（2）──────────────────────────── 用片語的插入譯成英文

584. 我即使有也很少上教堂做禮拜。
585. 他們的風俗習慣即使有不同，也很少。

586. 順便一提，你不需用刀子和叉子吃麵包。

587. 這項成功畢竟歸功於他的努力。
588. 令我大感驚訝的是，我發現他還活著。
589. 她的確是老了，不過很健康。
590. 我的老師可說是本活辭典。

"風俗習慣" 　586. *by the way* "順便一提" 　587. *after all* "畢竟"
be due to "歸功於" 　588. *to one's surprise* "令某人吃驚的是"
589. *to be sure , but ~* "的確，但是~" 　590. *so to speak* "可說是；好像"

（3）─────────────────────────────── 子句的插入

591. Mr. Lin is *what you call* a fine gentleman.

592. Night came on, and *what was worse*, we lost the way.

593. I will do whatever *you think* is proper.

594. What *do you think* he will propose to us?

595. He is a gentleman who *I believe* will help us in our work.

596. He came back to Taiwan two years later, *that is to say*, in 2005.

597. The newspaper is, *as it were*, the eyes and ears of society.

598. Japan, *as you all know*, is made up of four islands.

599. This is, *I am sure*, what he means.

600. He is not, *as far as I know*, a genius.

【註】591. *what you call* "你所謂的"　592. *what was worse* "更糟的是"
come on "來臨"　593. 的 you think 和 595. 的 I believe 為主要子句，
插在關係代名詞與動詞之間（詳見文法寶典 p. 164. 651）。　594. 為「疑問詞＋

（3）──────────────────────────── 子句的挿入

591. 林先生就是你所謂的高雅的紳士。

592. 夜晚來臨了，更糟的是，我們迷路了。

593. 我將做任何你認爲正當的事。

594. 你想他會向我們提議什麼？

595. 我相信他是在我們的工作方面，會有所幫助的人。

596. 他兩年以後回到台灣，那就是說，在二〇〇五年。

597. 報紙就好像是社會的眼睛和耳朵。

598. 衆所皆知的，日本是由四個島嶼所組成的。

599. 我確信這就是他的意思。

600. 就我所知，他不是個天才。

─────────────────────────────

do you think」所形成的疑問句，do you think 是主要子句，而不是挿入語
（詳見文法寶典 p.652）　　**597.** *as it were* "好像"　**598.** *be made up*
of ~ "由~組成"　　**600.** *as far as I know* "就我所知"

20. Inversion

（1）――――――――――――――――――――――― 副詞（片語）在句首的倒裝

601. *Never have I seen* such a charming girl.

602. *Not once* while I was in Washington *did I see* a traffic accident.

603. *Not until* I received a letter from her *did I know* that she had gone to America.

604. *Little did I dream* that I would be able to go to Africa.

605. *Hardly had he left* us when we burst out laughing.

606. *Only slowly did the boy understand* me.

607. *Only on Sunday does he get* a chance to go fishing.

（2）――――――――――――――――――――――― 受詞放在句首的倒裝

608. *That mountain* we are going to *climb.*

609. *Not a word did he speak* in my favor.

610. *What I am today* I *owe* to my parents.

【註】 601.～605.否定詞放在句首，主詞和助動詞要倒裝（詳見文法寶典 p.629.）。
602. …I did*n't* see a traffic accident *once.* 603. I did*n't* know
that she had gone to America *until* I received a letter from her.
604. I *little* dreamed that… (little = not at all) 605. *burst*
out + V-ing "突然～" 606.～607. 是普通的副詞片語放於句首的倒裝

20. 倒　裝　句

（1）───────────────────────── 副詞（片語）在句首的倒裝

601. 我從沒見過如此迷人的女孩。

602. 我在華盛頓的時候，從來沒見過一件交通事故。

603. 直到我收到了她寄來的一封信，才知道她已經去美國了。

604. 我幾乎沒有夢想過我能夠去非洲。

605. 他一離開我們，我們就大笑起來。

606. 那男孩很慢才瞭解我的話。

607. 只有在星期天，他才有機會去釣魚。

（2）───────────────────────── 受詞放在句首的倒裝

608. 那座山我們要去爬。

609. 他沒有為我說一句話。

610. 我之所以有今天，都要感謝我父母。

句。　607. *go fishing* "釣魚"　608.～610. 為受詞放在句首的倒裝。
608. We are going to climb *that* mountain.　609. He did *not* speak
a word… *in one's favor* "為了某人"　610. I owe *what I am to-*
day to my parents. *owe to*～ "感謝～"

（3）———————————————————————————— 補語的倒裝

611. *Happy is the man* who is contented.

612. *Poor* I *have been* and *poor* I *will always be.*

613. *Such was the shock* I gave her that she fell in a faint.

614. *So great was his disappointment* that he could not speak for a moment.

（4）———————————————————————————— 慣用語的倒裝

615. *May the Queen live* long !

616. " As to me, I have nothing particular to say. "
" *Nor（or Neither）do I.* "

617. " I will attend the party. " " *So will I.* "

618. *Go where you will*, you are sure to be welcomed.

619. *Young as Betty is*, she is intelligent.

620. *Should it rain* tomorrow, I will not go.

【註】 611.～ 614. 爲了使動詞與核心主詞接近，或強調補語，常把補語放在句首，而
將主詞與動詞倒裝。 613. *fall in a faint* "暈倒" 615. 爲祈願句的倒
裝＝*Long may* the Queen live ! 616. nor（*or* neither）用於句首時，主
詞和動詞須倒裝。 *as to*～ "關於～" 617. cf. " I am busy. " "*So am I.*"

（3）——————————————————————————— 補語的倒裝

611. 知足者常樂。

612. 我一直很窮，而且永遠會這麼窮。

613. 我給她如此大的打擊，因此她暈倒了。

614. 他是如此失望，因此一時說不出話來。

（4）——————————————————————————— 慣用語的倒裝

615. 祝皇后萬歲！

616. 「關於我，我沒什麼特別要說的。」
　　　「我也是。」

617. 「我將要參加宴會。」「我也要參加。」

618. 不論你到哪裏，一定會受歡迎的。

619. 雖然貝蒂那麼年輕，她却是聰明的。

620. 如果明天下雨，我就不去。

（我也是。）" You are busy." *"So am I."*（是的，我很忙。）(cf.
646.)　618.=Wherever you may go,…=No matter where you may
go,…（cf.338.和343.）*be sure to* "一定"　619. = Though Betty is
young,…（cf.326.）　620.=If it should rain tomorrow,…

21. Apposition

（1）————————————————————————— 用同位格片語把句子譯成英文

621. *Graham Bell*, *an American scientist*, invented the telephone.

622. He had to give up his favorite *pastime —reading*.

623. Ben had *the kindness to write a letter* of recommendation.

624. He has *no wish to be chairman*.

625. She proposed *the idea* of *contributing money to relieving the poor*.

626. *The news* of *his sudden death* has greatly surprised us.

（2）————————————————————————— 用同位語子句把句子譯成英文

627. *The fact that we are inclined to accept conventional forms as the correct ones* is beyond dispute.

628. There is *an old saying that everybody's business is nobody's business*.

629. I will see to *it that the work is done in time*.

630. I think *it* natural *that everything should be done in accordance with the rules*.

【註】 621. Graham Bell 和 an American scientist 是同位語。　622. reading 在說明 pastime。　*give up* "放棄"　623.624.的不定詞是前面名詞的同位語，用來說明該名詞。　625.和 626.為「名詞＋of＋名詞」的型式。同位語用來說明 of 前面的名詞。　625. *contribute ～ to …* "捐助～給…"

21. 同　位　語

（1）――――――――――――――――――― 用同位格片語把句子譯成英文

621. 一位美國的科學家，格雷姆・貝爾，發明了電話。

622. 他必須放棄他最喜歡的消遣――閱讀。

623. 班很好意地寫了一封介紹信。

624. 他並不想當主席。

625. 她提出捐錢救濟貧民的想法。

626. 他突然過世的消息，令我們非常驚訝。

（2）――――――――――――――――――― 用同位語子句把句子譯成英文

627. 我們傾向於承認傳統形式是正確的事實，不容置疑。

628. 有句古老諺語說：「衆人事，沒人做。」

629. 我會留意及時做好那工作。

630. 每件事都該根據規則來做，我認爲這是自然的。

627.和 628.的 that 子句用來說明前面的 the fact 和 an old saying 的內容。

629.和 630.的 that 子句爲眞正受詞，it 爲形式受詞（詳見文法寶典 p.114）

629. see（to it）*that*～　"留意必定～"

22. Common Relation

631. *Early to rise* and *early to bed* **makes** a man healthy.

632. The birds were all busily *searching for* and *pursuing* **the insects**.

633. Linda *was*, *is*, and *will be*, **your true friend**.

634. Speech *is*, or *should be*, **silver**, but silence is gold.

635. He *has been* and always *will be* **delicate**.

636. The greater part of our activity *is*, and *must be*, **based** upon tradition.

637. This boat carries people to the island *from*, and takes them back *to*, **the wharf**.

638. Effort is as precious *as*, and perhaps more precious *than*, **the work** it results in.

639. Democracy is *the government of the people*, *by the people*, and *for the people*.

640. It seems to me that *a man who has much money*, but *who has a mean character* is not happy.

【註】（A＋B）X 和 X（A＋B）的 X 表示 A 和 B 所共用的字詞。 631. Early to rise and early to bed 等於 A＋B，為完全主詞，在此情況要用單數動詞。 632. *search for* "尋找" 634. Speech is silver, silence is golden. "說話是銀，沉默是金"〔諺〕 636. *be based on* ～ "以～為基礎"

22. 共用關係

（1）──────────────────（A＋B）X 的關係

631. 早睡早起使一個人健康。
632. 鳥兒們當時都忙著尋找和追捕昆蟲。

633. 琳達過去是，現在是，將來也是你的眞正朋友。
634. 說話是銀，或許應該是銀，而沉默却是金。
635. 他一直是，也將永遠是脆弱的。
636. 我們活動的大部分是，也必須是，以傳統爲基礎。

637. 這艘船載人從碼頭到島上，並載他們回到碼頭。

638. 努力和它所導致的成果一樣珍貴，或許更珍貴。

（2）──────────────────X（A＋B）的關係

639. 民主政治就是民有、民治、民享的政府。

640. 我想一個很有錢，却有著卑劣人格的人，是不快樂的。

---

637. *take back* "回到"　　638. *result in* "導致"　　639. of the people,
by the people, for the people 共同修飾 government。　　640. who 所引
導的形容詞子句，修飾 man。a man of character "有人格的人"

23. Substitute

（1）──────────────────────────────── **do** 的代用

641. I love Richard more than you *do*.

642. You know more than I *did* at your age.

643. "Who do you say suffered from rheumatism?"
"I say Father *did*."

644. If Heaven did not send the young gentleman to us,
who *did*?

645. He had promised to stop smoking, but he failed to
do so.

646. "You often make mistakes." "So I *do*; but so *does*
everybody."

（2）──────────────────────────── 代名詞、副詞的代用

647. His behavior is not *that* of a gentleman.

648. Compare your composition with *those* of your friends.

649. These gloves are too large. Do you have any smaller
ones?

650. "Is Brenda conscious of her own faults?"
"No, I don't think *so*."

【註】641. do = love him　642. did = knew　643. did = suffered from
rheumatism　*suffer from*～ "患～病"　644. did = sent him to
us　645. do so = stop smoking　*fail to*～ "沒有～"　646. So I
do.= Yes, I do.　so does everybody = everybody often makes mis-

23. 代　用　語

（1）────────────────────────── **do** 的代用

641. 我比你愛理查。

642. 你所懂的，比我在你這個年紀時懂的還多。

643. 「你說誰患了風濕？」
　　　「我說父親。」

644. 如果不是上帝賜給我們這個年輕人，會是誰呢？

645. 他答應戒煙的，不過沒有做到。

646. 「你時常犯錯。」「我是常犯錯，不過每個人都這樣。」

（2）────────────────────────── 代名詞、副詞的代用

647. 他的行為不是個君子的行為。

648. 把你的作文和你朋友的比較一下。

649. 這些手套太大了，你有沒有小一點的？

650. 「布蘭德知道她自己的錯誤嗎？」
　　　「不，我想她不知道。」

---

takes, too. (cf. 617)　　647. that = the behavior　　648. those =
the compositions　　*compare ～with* … "把～和…比較"　　649. ones
＝gloves　　650. so = she is conscious of her own faults.

24. Emphasis

（1）———————————————————————————字詞的強調

651. A car stopped *right in front of* my house last night.

652. This is the *very book* our teacher frequently refers to.

653. The *very day* school started, Tom came down with the measles.

654. You have to try *every possible* means.

655. The car was running at the *highest possible* speed.

656. Can I *ever* forget that dreadful scene?

657. *Nothing whatever* was found in the box.

658. He asked me *what in the world* made me do that contrary to his expectations.

659. *What on earth* happened during my absence?

660. I'm *not in the least* interested in what you have said.

【註】 651. right = just，用來強調 in front of "在～前面"　652. 和 653. 的
very 有形容詞的意味，強調後面的名詞。　652. *refer to* "提到"
653. *come down with*～ "因～而病倒"　654. 和 655. possible 前面以
every, all，或最高級來強調。　656. 為一反語。　657. whatever 強調否定

24. 強調構句

651. 昨晚一輛車子就停在我家前面。

652. 這本就是我們老師時常向我們提到的書。

653. 就在學校開學的那天，湯姆因麻疹而病倒了。

654. 你應該嘗試每一種可能的方法。

655. 當時那輛車正以最快速度急駛著。

656. 我忘得了那可怕的情景嗎？

657. 那個盒子裏什麼都沒有。

658. 他問我倒底是什麼，使我做出和他期望相違的事情。

659. 我不在時，到底發生了什麼事？

660. 我對你所說的，一點兒也不感興趣。

意思，等於 at all。　658.和 659. *in the world* 和 *on earth* 強調疑問詞，有"到底"的意思。　658. *contrary to* ～　"和～相反"　659. *during one's absence* "某人不在時"　660. *not in the least* = *not at all* "一點也不"

（2）————————————————————————————— **do** 的強調

661. *Do come* to see us next Sunday.

662. *Do enjoy* yourself here in New York.

663. He doesn't talk much, but when he *does talk*, he always speaks to the point.

664. She said she would come and she *did come*.

665. Fred *did love* me once, but he loves me no longer.

（3）————————————————————————————— 反身代名詞的強調

666. I didn't see *the man himself*, but they say he is *kindness itself*.

（4）————————————————————————————— 否定字的強調

667. *Never did I think* that Taiwan would make such a remarkable progress in industry after the recovery.

（5）————————————————————————————— 重覆字詞的強調

668. They walked *on and on* along the river.

669. She read it *over and over* again, till she learned it all by heart.

670. We *talked and talked* until late at night.

【註】661.～665. 用 do 來加強語氣，強調動詞、狀態的眞實性，或實現的程度等。

662. *enjoy oneself* "盡情玩樂" 663. *to the point* "切題" 665. *no longer* "不再" 666. 在名詞的後面接 -self 的形式，表示強調那個名詞。

667. 將 not 或 never 等否定句放於句首，句子倒裝，用來強調其意（參照 601

（2）——————————————————————————— do 的強調

661. 下星期日一定要來看我們。
662. 在紐約這兒一定要盡情玩樂。
663. 他很少說話，不過他一說話時，總是講得很切題。

664. 她說她會來，而且眞的來了。
665. 弗雷德確實曾經愛過我，不過不再愛我了。

（3）——————————————————————— 反身代名詞的強調

666. 我沒見到那個人本人，不過據說他很親切。

（4）————————————————————————— 否定字的強調

667. 我從來沒想到台灣在光復後，工業會有如此驚人的進步。

（5）——————————————————————— 重覆字詞的強調

668. 他們沿著河一直走。
669. 她一遍又一遍地讀它，直到全部背起來。

670. 我們一直談到深夜。

───

〔註〕661.～674. 通是用 It is ~ that 之強調句型（詳見動詞篇
～605.）　668.和669.的 *on and on* "一直地"，*over and over* "一遍又
一遍"均為強調的副詞。　669. *learn ~ by heart* "背～"　670. 動詞重覆
亦為強調意味。　*late at night* "深夜"

（6）————————————————————It is ～ that的強調構句

671. *It is in this cottage that* the great scientist was born.

672. *It was during World War* Ⅱ *that* I got acquainted with Earnest.

673. *It is* a foolish bird *that* soils its own nest.

674. *It was not until I got home that* I noticed the loss of my purse.

675. *What is it that* you want me to do?

676. *Why is it that* people should seldom visit such a beautiful place?

677. As a matter of fact *it is I who* am likely to drop behind the hikers.

678. *It is you*, *not he*, *who* are worthy of praise.

（7）————————————————————疑問句的強調

679. *Who knows* what will happen tomorrow?

680. *Who can master* English without working hard?

【註】671.～674. 強調 it is 和 that 之間的語句。去掉 it is 和 that 時，就是普通的句子：671. In this cottage the great scientist was born.　672.During World War Ⅱ I got acquainted with Earnest.　*get acquainted with*～ " 認識～ "　674. It is not until ～ that … " 直到～才… "
675. 和 676. 「疑問詞＋is it that」的句型，強調疑問詞。　677.和678. It

(6) ─────────────────────────── **It is ～ that** 的強調構句

671. 那位偉大的科學家，就在這間茅屋裏誕生了。

672. 就在二次世界大戰期間，我認識了俄尼斯特。

673. 笨鳥才弄髒自己的巢。〔諺〕

674. 我回到家才發現我的錢包掉了。

675. 你要我做的是什麼？

676. 爲什麼人們竟很少參觀這麼一個美麗的地方？

677. 事實上可能落在徒步旅行者後面的人是我。

678. 是你值得稱讚，而不是他。

(7) ─────────────────────────── 疑問句的強調

679. 誰知道明天會發生什麼？

680. 有誰能不努力用功就精通英文的？

---

is ～ that … 的 that 指人時，可用 who 代替。　677. *as a matter of fact*
"事實上" *be likely to* "可能" *drop behind* "落後" 678. *worthy*
of "值得" 679. 680. 用疑問句強調，是修辭疑問句，有「究竟～；難道～」
的意思。

25. Negation

681. You must *not* keep him waiting so long.

682. You should *not* look down upon a man because he is *not* rich.

683. The prices are tending to go on rising, and I *can't* afford to keep a car.

684. Who does *not* know it ?

685. *Not a few* people are killed in traffic accidents every year.

686. *Not many of them* paid any attention to it.

687. *Not* a drop of rain has fallen for the last two months.

688. I *don't* think Barbara agreed with you.

689. " Will you be back by two o'clock ? "

   " Well, *I'm afraid not* . "

690. " Do we have a test in English today ? "

   " I *hope not* . "

【註】682. *look down upon* "輕視"　　683. *tend to* ～ "有～的傾向"
afford to "力足以"　　684.＝Everybody knows it.　　685. *not a*
few＝many　　686. *not many*＝few　　*pay attention to* ～ "注意～"

25. 否定構句

681. 你不可以讓他等這麼久。

682. 你不應該因爲一個人沒有錢就輕視他。

683. 物價有繼續上漲的傾向，所以我負擔不了一部車子。

684. 誰不知道那件事？

685. 每年都有不少人在交通事故中喪生。

686. 他們之中沒有多少人注意到它。

687. 上兩個月沒有下過一滴雨。

688. 我認爲芭芭拉不會同意你。

689. 「你兩點以前會回來嗎？」

　　　「嗯，恐怕不會。」

690. 「我們今天有英文測驗嗎？」

　　　「希望沒有。」

---

687. not 放句首，表強調。　688. 意思是 I think Barbara did*n't* agree with you. *agree with*＋*sb.* "同意某人"　690. 意思是 I hope we do*n't* have a test … ＝ I do*n't* hope we have a test …

（2）———————————————————————— **no** 的用法

691. *No one* can express the beauty of the scenery by means of words.

692. My friend gave me *no ink*, so I could write *no more*.

693. There was *no one* who didn't feel pity for the orphan.

694. Robert is *no poet*. He hardly understands what is beautiful.

695. I was very tired and could walk *no farther*.

（3）———————————————————————— **neither** 的用法

696. *Neither of the two* watches shows the correct time.

697. He didn't know how to solve the problem, and *neither did I*.

（4）———————————————————————— **nobody , none , nothing** 的用法

698. *Nobody* came to see me unusually last Sunday.

699. According to the newspaper, *none* of the people helped the man on the platform.

700. I have *nothing* more to say.

【註】691. no one 作主詞。 此句＝ Anyone can't express … *by means of*
" 藉著 "　　693. *feel pity for* " 同情 "　　694. no 為否定的強調。
696.697. neither 是全部否定。　　696. neither 為一單數的代名詞，所以後

（2）──────────────────────── **no** 的用法

691. 沒有人能夠用言語表達那景色之美。

692. 我的朋友沒給我墨水，所以我不能再寫了。

693. 沒有人不同情孤兒。

694. 羅伯特根本不是個詩人。他幾乎不懂得什麼是美。

695. 我非常疲倦，再也走不動了。

（3）──────────────────────── **neither** 的用法

696. 這兩隻錶都不準。

697. 他不知道如何解決這個問題，我也不知道。

（4）────────────────── **nobody , none , nothing** 的用法

698. 上星期天很不尋常地，沒有人來看我。

699. 根據報紙報導，沒有人幫助在月台上的那個人。

700. 我沒什麼好說了。

───────────────────────────────────

面動詞要用單數。　697. Neither did I.≒ I didn't know, either.
698. nobody = no one　699. *according to* "根據"　700. = I don't
have anything more to say.

（5）———————————————— scarcely , seldom , little , few的用法

701. For a while we could *scarcely* hear anything.

702. It is *seldom* that such things happen at the same time.

703. Tom is accustomed to drinking *little coffee* at home.

704. *Few students* think that the school playground is large in comparison with that in the park.

（6）———————————————————— 部分否定

705. A talented man does *not always* succeed in life.

706. I did*n't* understand *all* of his speech.

707. *Both* of his parents are *not* alive.

708. This butterfly is *not* to be found *everywhere* in Australia.

709. Smart students do *not necessarily* become good teachers.

710. The news you heard is *not altogether* false.

【註】 701. scarcely ～＝ hardly ～ "幾乎～都沒有" hardly 較常用，這兩個字都常和 can 一起使用。 *for a while* "一時" 702. seldom～＝ rarely～ "不常；很少" *at the same time* "同時" 703. *be accustomed to*＋ V-ing "習慣～" 704. *in comparison with* "和～相比" 705.～ 710.都是部分否定的形式，其完全否定比較如下： 705. *cf.* A talented man

(5) ———————————————————scarcely , seldom , little , few 的用法

701. 一時我們幾乎什麼都聽不到 。

702. 這樣的事情很少同時發生 。

703. 湯姆在家習慣很少喝咖啡 。

704. 和公園的運動場比起來 ，很少學生認為學校的運動場是大的 。

(6) ———————————————————————部分否定

705. 一個有才幹的人 ，一生中未必成功 。

706. 並非他所有的演講我都了解 。

707. 他的父母並不是都活著 。

708. 這種蝴蝶並不是在澳洲的每個地方都看得到 。

709. 聰明的學生不一定都成為好老師 。

710. 你聽到的消息並非完全是假的 。

---

never succeeds ···　706. *cf.* I didn't understand any of his speech.
707. *cf.* Neither of his parents is (*or* are) alive.　708. *cf.* This
butterfly is to be found nowhere in Australia.　709. *not neces-*
sarily "不一定"　710. *not altogether* "並非完全"

(7) ———————————————————————————— 否定的慣用語

711. You *cannot* be *too* careful in the choice of your friends.

712. We do *not* appreciate the value of health *until* we lose it.

(8) ———————————————————————————— 雙重否定

713. I *cannot* visit this place *without* being reminded of my happy old days.

714. *Not* a day passed *but* he wrote to me.

(9) ———————————————————————————— 否定意味的肯定句

715. He is *far from* wise. I have never seen a man so silly as he.

716. "My room is *anything but* clean." "So is mine."

717. He is *the last* person who would be accused of taking bribes.

718. Mary hung up the telephone *before* I had finished talking.

719. His argument is *above* my understanding.

720. The patient is quite *beyond* recovery.

【註】 711. *cannot ～ too* … "再…都不爲過" *in the choice of ～* "選擇～方面" 712. *not ～until* … "直到…才～" 713. = Whenever I visit this place, it reminds me of my happy old days. remind … of ～ "使…想起～" 714.「否定＋否定」→「肯定」 715. *far from ～* =

（7）───────────────────────────── 否定的慣用語

711. 在選擇朋友方面，再小心也不為過。

712. 我們一直到失去了健康，才了解健康的重要性。

（8）───────────────────────────── 雙重否定

713. 我每次遊歷此地，總是想起我快樂的往日。

714. 他沒有一天不寫信給我。

（9）───────────────────────────── 否定意味的肯定句

715. 他一點也不聰明。我從來沒見過像他這麼愚笨的人。

716.「我的房間很不乾淨。」「我的也是。」
717. 他是最不可能被控告受賄賂的人。

718. 我還沒講完話，瑪麗就把電話掛了。

719. 他的理由我聽不懂。
720. 這病患無法復元了。

---

anything but ～ " 一點也不 "　717. *the last* ～ " 最不可能的 "　*be accused of* " 被控告 " *take a bribe* " 收取賄賂 "　718. *hang up* " 掛斷電話 "（相反詞 *hang on* " 不掛電話 "）　719. 720. above ～ = beyond ～ " 為～所不及；非～能力所及 "

26. **Inanimate Subject**

(1)———————————————— 用 **make , cause , enable , help** 等動詞

721. ***The careful reading of this book*** will *make* you an expert at skiing.

722. ***A glance at the weather*** *made* her pedal her bicycle hurriedly.

723. ***What*** *caused* Donald to change his mind ?

724. ***Airplanes*** *enable* us to arrive in Paris in a day.

725. ***Machines*** *help* us work with greater ease.

(2)———————————————————— 用 **allow , compel** 等動詞

726. ***Her pride*** did not *allow* her to do anything dishonorable.

727. ***The stormy weather*** *compelled* us to postpone our departure.

(3)——————————————————— 用 **take, bring, lead** 等動詞

728. ***This bus*** will *take* you to the university you are *looking for*.

729. ***Hunger*** seems to *have brought* the bear to our village.

730. ***This book*** *leads* to a good knowledge of the life in France.

【註】 721. ～725. make, cause , enable, help 都有使役的意味。　721. = If you read this book carefully, you will become an expert Go-player. 722. = When she glanced at the weather, she pedaled her bicycle hurriedly. 724. = We can arrive in Paris in a day by airplanes.

26. 無生物當主詞的構句

（1）─────────────────── 用 **make , cause , enable , help** 等動詞

721. 仔細閱讀這本書，將使你成爲滑雪專家。

722. 她看了一下天氣，便匆匆地踩她的脚踏車。

723. 是什麼使唐諾德改變了心意？

724. 飛機使我們能在一天之內到達巴黎。

725. 機器幫助我們更輕易地工作。

（2）─────────────────── 用 **allow , compel** 等動詞

726. 她的自尊心不容許她做任何不名譽的事。

727. 暴風雨天迫使我們延期出發。

（3）─────────────────── 用 **take , bring , lead** 等動詞

728. 這輛公共汽車會載你到你正在找的大學去。

729. 飢餓似乎使那隻熊到我們村落來。

730. 這本書能使人清楚地了解法國的生活。

---

enable ～to…" 使～能…" 　725.*with ease* "輕易地" 　726.727. allow, compel＋*sb.*＋不定詞　726.＝She was too proud to do anything dishonorable.　727. We had to postpone our departure because of the stormy weather.　728.＝If you take this bus, you can get to the university.

（4）—————————————————————— 用 **prevent, keep** 等動詞

731. *The storm* *prevented* the ship from leaving port.
732. *A traffic accident* *kept* me from getting to the airport on time.

（5）—————————————————————— 用 **keep, leave** 等動詞

733. *Extra work* *kept* them at the factory until seven.
734. *The payment of his debts* *left* him penniless.

（6）—————————————————————— 用 **remind, deprive** 等動詞

735. *The sunrise* always *reminds* me *of* the scenery of my native place.
736. *Astonishment* almost *deprived* the girl *of* her speech.

（7）—————————————————————— 用 **give, show, cost, surprise** 等動詞

737. *The situation of our house* *gives* us the view of the whole valley.
738. *A careful comparison* will *show* you the difference between two languages.
739. *Carelessness with fire* *cost* John his life.
740. *Nancy's denial of the fact* *surprised* me very much.

【註】731.732. *prevent, keep ~ from* … "阻止~做…"（詳見文法寶典 p. 280）
731. = The ship could not leave port owing to the storm. 732. *get*
to "到達" 733. They were at the factory until seven because of extra work. 734. He was penniless because he payed his debts.
735. *remind ~ of* … "使~想起…" 736. *deprive ~ of* … "剝奪~

（4）──────────────────── 用 **prevent**，**keep** 等動詞

731. 暴風雨使得那艘船無法離港。

732. 一件交通事故使我無法準時到達機場。

（5）──────────────────── 用 **keep**，**leave** 等動詞

733. 加班使他們在工廠待到七點。

734. 償債使他一文不名。

（6）──────────────────── 用 **remind**，**deprive** 等動詞

735. 日出總是使我想起我故鄉的風景。

736. 驚訝使那女孩說不出話來。

（7）──────────────────── 用 **give**，**show**，**cost**，**surprise** 等動詞

737. 我們房子的位置使我們能夠眺望整個山谷。

738. 仔細的比較將告訴你兩種語言的不同。

739. 對火的大意使得約翰喪失了生命。

740. 南西對事實的否認，令我非常驚訝。

的…" 此句＝The girl was so much astonished that she could hardly
speak.　738.＝Compare two languages carefully, and you will see
the difference.　739.＝John lost his life through carelessness with
fire.　740.＝To my great surprise, Nancy denied the fact.

27. Noun Construction

(1) ─────────────────────────── 名詞＋**of**＋名詞

741. *The invention of radio* has changed the world.

742. *The knowledge of his safe arrival* delighted his family.

743. You are welcome to *the use of my typewriter*.

744. He told me of *his wife's love of flowers*.

745. He is the *designer of this hotel*.

746. Helen made a detailed *description of the scene*.

(2) ─────────────────────── 名詞＋**of** 以外的介系詞＋名詞

747. Jimmy paid *a visit to Rome*.

748. He has a strong *resemblance to his father*.

749. On *my entrance into the theater*, the play was about to start.

750. *His succession to Mr. Brown* as manager is rather an unexpected piece of news.

───

【註】 741. invented radio → the invention of radio   743. *be welcome to* ～ "可隨意～"   744. his wife loved flowers → his wife's love of flowers   745. he designs this hotel → the designer of this hotel
747. visited Rome → a visit to Rome   *pay a visit to* ～ "遊覽 ～"

27. 名詞片語

（1）——————————————————————————————— 名詞＋**of**＋名詞

741. 收音機的發明改變了世界。

742. 他安全抵達的消息，使他的家人很高興。

743. 你可隨意用我的打字機。

744. 他告訴我他太太喜愛花。

745. 他是這家飯店的設計人。

746. 海倫對實況做了一個詳細的描述。

（2）—————————————————————— 名詞＋**of** 以外的介系詞＋名詞

747. 吉米遊覽了羅馬。

748. 他很像他父親。

749. 我進入戲院時，戲正要開始。

750. 他繼任布朗先生當經理，實在是件非常出人意料之外的新聞。

---

748. he resembles his father → resemblance to his father　749. I entered the theater → my entrance into the theater　*be about to*＋V
"正要～"　750. he succeeds Mr. Brown → his succession to Mr. Brown

（3）————————————————————————— 名詞＋不定詞

751. *Mr. Hill's decision to retire* surprised all of us.

752. He persisted in *his refusal to attend* the conference.

753. Tom has *the ability to make* a rational plan.

754. Mary couldn't withstand *the curiosity to look into* the fact of the case.

755. He has *the courage to speak out* what he thinks is right.

（4）————————————————————— 形容詞轉化成的名詞＋介詞＋名詞

756. *Ignorance of this law* does not excuse you.

757. Some students found *difficulty in solving* the problem.

758. There is at present a *serious shortage of oil*.

759. We could not decide upon it owing to *the chairman's absence from the meeting*.

760. *His freedom from official duties* made it possible for him to continue his study.

【註】 751.752.是由及物動詞＋不定詞轉化成的名詞＋不定詞。751. Mr. Hill decided to retire→Mr. Hill's decision to retire　752. *persist in* " 堅持 " 753.～755.是形容詞＋不定詞轉化成的名詞＋不定詞。 753.＝Tom is able to make a rational plan.　754. *look into* "調查"　755.＝He is courageous to speak out… *speak out* "說出"　756.＝If you are ignorant of this law,

（3）───────────────────────── 名詞＋不定詞

751. 希爾先生的決定退休，令我們大家非常驚訝。

752. 他堅持不參加那會議。

753. 湯姆有能力擬定一個合理的計畫。

754. 瑪麗耐不住要調查這問題眞相的好奇心。

755. 他有勇氣說出他認爲對的事情。

（4）───────────────── 形容詞轉化成的名詞＋介詞＋名詞

756. 不知法律也不能使你免罪。

757. 有些學生發現解決那個問題有困難。

758. 目前石油嚴重匱乏。

759. 因爲主席沒來開會，所以我們不能決定那件事。

760. 他因爲沒有公務而能繼續他的研究。

---

you are not excused.　757.＝Some students found it difficult to solve the problem.　758.＝We are at present seriously short of oil. *at present* "目前"　759.＝…because the chairman was absent from the meeting. *decide* (*up*)*on*～ "決定～"　760.＝He was able to continue his study because he was free from official duties. *free from* ～ "沒有～"

(5)──────────────────────────── 名詞＋介系詞＋名詞

761. Nancy paid little *attention to my advice*.

762. *His sudden death from cancer* surprised us very much.

763. My uncle is *a dealer in rice*.

764. They are glad of *your success in the attempt*.

765. On his *arrival at the station* he called a taxi.

766. Her *recovery from the illness* is past all hope.

(6)──────────────────────────── 動詞＋形容詞＋名詞

767. I *had a good sleep* last night.

768. He *gave me a shy nod*.

769. He is *a habitual liar*.

770. He is *a great lover* of surfing.

【註】761.～766. 不及物動詞＋介系詞＋名詞可改爲"名詞＋介系詞＋名詞"的型式。
761.＝Nancy attended to my advice very little. *pay attention to* "注
意" 762.＝We were very surprised that he died from cancer. 763.My
uncle deals in rice. a dealer in ～ "～商人" 764.＝They are glad
that you have succeeded in the attempt. *be glad of*～ "高興～"

（5）————————————————— 名詞＋介系詞＋名詞

761. 南西不注意我的忠告。

762. 他突然死於癌症，令我們非常驚訝。

763. 我叔父是個米商。

764. 他們很高興你的嘗試成功。

765. 他一到達車站，就叫了部計程車。

766. 她要從病中康復是絕無希望的。

（6）————————————————— 動詞＋形容詞＋名詞

767. 我昨晚睡得很好。

768. 他羞怯地向我點個頭。

769. 他慣於說謊。

770. 他非常喜歡衝浪。

765.＝When he arrived at the station… 766.＝It is past all hope that she will recover from the illness. *past all hope* "絕無希望" 767.～ 770. "動詞（或be）＋形容詞＋名詞"時，在名詞前面的形容詞，意義上可作副詞。和 767. 768. 類似的有 take a comfortable trip, make a rude reply 等；和 769. 770. 類似的有 a good swimmer, a hard worker, an early riser 等。

28. Correlative

（1）──────────────────────────────── 相關代名詞

771. David's brothers are both overseas ; *one* in Brazil, and *the other* in Spain.
772. Reading is easy, and thinking is hard work, but *the one* is useless without *the other*.
773. To know is *one thing*, to practice is *another*.
774. In our university *some* of the students speak English and *others* speak Spanish.

（2）──────────────────────────────── 相關連接詞

775. Thanks to the radio, we can enjoy *both* the world news *and* its greatest music in our homes.
776. I found this book was *not only* interesting *but also* instructive.
777. *Either* he *or* I am responsible for the consequence.
778. I like fall, for it is *neither* too cold *nor* too warm.
779. I went to Taipei *not that* I wanted to see Jane, *but that* I loved the city.
780. *It is true* Margaret is young, *but* she is prudent for her age.

【註】771.～774. 為相關代名詞　771. *one ~ the other*… "（二者）一個~，另一個…"　772. *the one ~ the other* … = *the former ~ the latter*… "前者~，後者…"　773. *~one thing*, …*another* "（二者）~是一回事，…是另一回事"　774. some~others… "有些~，有些…"　775.～780. 相關連接詞　775. *both* A *and* B "A和B都"　*thanks to*~ "由於~"　776. *not only* A *but* (*also*)

28. 相關詞構句

（1）――――――――――――――――――――――――――― 相關代名詞

771. 大衞的兩個兄弟都在國外；一個在巴西，另一個在西班牙。

772. 閱讀容易，思考困難，不過其中一個沒有了另一個就沒用。

773. 知道是一回事，實行又是另一回事。

774. 在我們的大學中，有些學生說英文，有些說西班牙文。

（2）――――――――――――――――――――――――――― 相關連接詞

775. 由於有收音機，我們才能在家中欣賞世界新聞和最了不起的音樂。

776. 我發覺這本書不但有趣，而且還有教育性。

777. 不是他就是我負責這後果。

778. 我喜歡秋天，因爲它不太冷也不太熱。

779. 我到台北不是因爲要看珍，而是我喜歡那個都市。

780. 瑪格麗特確實很年輕，不過以她的年齡而言，她是非常精明謹慎的。

B "不但A，而且B" 777. *either* A *or* B "不是A，就是B" *be respon-sible for* ～ "負責～" 778. *neither* A *nor* B "不是A，也不是B" 注意 776.～778.的動詞和B一致。 779. *not that* ～*but that* … "不是因爲～，而是因爲 …"，that＝because 780. It is true ～but … ＝ Indeed ～but … *for one's age* "以某人的年齡而言"

29. Narration

781. Michael said, " Liberal education is an odd phrase in itself. "

782. She said to me, " The watch my uncle gave me keeps good time. "

783. The clerk said to me, " Do you have any change ? "

784. Mr. Lin said to me, " Was your father at home yesterday ? "

785. Yesterday he said to her, " Why didn't you call on me yesterday ? "

786. Mr. Wang said to me, " Be quiet and attend to me. "

787. The teacher said, " Let's add some salt to it. "

788. The teacher said to us, " Don't make fun of his English. He is doing the best he can. "

789. Mother said to me, " You look pale. What's the matter with you ? "

790. Anne said, " There is something wrong with the telephone. I cannot make myself heard at all. "

【註】 781. =Michael said liberal education was an odd phrase in itself.
782. = She told me (*that*) the watch her uncle had given her kept good time. 783. =The clerk asked me if I had some change.
784. Mr. Lin asked me if my father had been at home the day before. 785. =Yesterday he asked her why she hadn't called on him

29. 敘 述 法

直接敘述法

781. 麥克說：「自由教育本身就是個奇特的措詞。」

782. 她對我說：「我叔父給我的手錶很準。」

783. 那個店員對我說：「你有零錢嗎？」

784. 林先生對我說：「你父親昨天在家嗎？」

785. 昨天他對她說：「妳昨天為什麼不來看我？」

786. 王先生對我說：「安靜點，注意我說的話。」

787. 老師說：「讓我們給它加點鹽。」

788. 老師對我們說：「不要取笑他的英文，他正在盡最大努力。」

789. 媽媽對我說：「你看起來臉色蒼白。你怎麼啦？」

790. 安說：「這電話有點毛病，我的話對方一點也聽不到。」

---

the day before yesterday. 786.＝Mr. Wang told me to be quiet and to attend to him. 787.＝The teacher suggested that we should add some salt to it. 788.＝The teacher told us not to make fun of his English because he was doing the best he could. 789.＝Mother told me that I looked pale and asked what was the matter with me.

30. Colloquial English

———————————————— 常用的口語英文

791. " I have a terrible headache. " " That's too bad. Let me feel your pulse. "

792. " Hello. I'd like some information about the entrance examination. " " Hold the line, please. "

793. " Excuse me, but can you tell me the way to the Sing Sheng Theater ? " " Yes, certainly. "

794. " Excuse me, but where is Taipei Station ? " " I beg your pardon ? Please speak more slowly."

795. " Can I try this coat on ? I like it very much. How much is it ? " " Well, it's only 600 dollars. "

796. " How about some more coffee ? " " No, thank you. I've had enough. "

797. " How about playing tennis this afternoon ? " " Why not ! "

798. " Do you mind if I smoke ? " " No, I don't. "

799. " Sorry, I couldn't be of much help to you. " " Thank you all the same. "

800. " If you see David, say hello to him for me. " " All right. I will. "

【註】791. 有關健康的口語：I have caught a bad cold. "我得了重感冒。" Take care of yourself. "請保重。" 792. 電話中口語：(*This is*)Miss Brown speaking. "我是布朗小姐。" Who's calling, please ? "請問是哪位 ? " You have the wrong number. "你打錯電話了。" 793. 問路時口語：Let me draw you a map. "我畫張地圖給你。" I'm a stranger here

30. 會話英文

791. 「我頭痛得很厲害。」「眞糟糕，我來替你把把脈。」

792. 「喂。我想要一些入學考試的資料。」「請稍等。」

793. 「對不起，你能告訴我到新聲戲院的路嗎？」
　　「好的，當然好。」

794. 「對不起，台北車站在哪裏？」
　　「再說一次好嗎？請說慢一點。」

795. 「我能試穿這件外套嗎？我非常喜歡它。多少錢？」
　　「嗯，只要六百元。」

796. 「再來點咖啡好嗎？」
　　「不了，謝謝你，我吃夠了。」

797. 「今天下午去打網球好嗎？」
　　「好啊！」

798. 「你介意我抽煙嗎？」「不，我不介意。」

799. 「對不起，我無法幫很多忙。」
　　「還是一樣謝謝你。」

800. 「如果你看到大衞，替我向他問好。」
　　「好的，我會的。」

---

myself. "這裏我自己也不熟。" 794. I beg your pardon？ 句尾音調上揚，表示聽不清對方的話，請再說一次的意思。 796. 若接受建議，則說 Yes, please. 797. Why not！的意思就等於 Yes, let's. I'd love to. 798."不介意"也可用 Not in the least. 800. say hello to him for me = give my best regards to him

Test 1

1. 我們必須尊敬長者。

_____

2. 這一篇文章值得仔細閱讀。

_____

3. 張先生去年去了日本，就再無消息。

_____

4. 我必須在臺灣銀行開一個帳戶。

_____

5. He indicated approval with a nod.

_____

6. The sun keeps us warm.

_____

7. Swimming can make us strong.

_____

8. The flowers were kept fresh and green.

_____

【解答】

1. We must respect our elders.　2. This article is worth reading carefully.　3. We haven't heard of Mr. Chang since he went to Japan last year.　4. I must open an account with Bank of Taiwan.　5. 他點頭表示贊同。　6. 太陽使我們溫暖。　7. 游泳能使我們強壯。　8. 花被保持著新鮮嫩綠。

Test 2

1. 中國字很難寫嗎？

_____

2. 那一位戴黃帽子的外國人是誰？

_____

3. 請問，到台北火車站怎麼走？

_____

4. 你有記日記的習慣嗎？

_____

5. They often keep late hours.

_____

6. Her watch has been stolen.

_____

7. The policeman pushed the door open.

_____

8. An idler always finds time heavy on his hands.

_____

【解答】

1. Are Chinese characters difficult〔hard〕to write？　2. Who is that foreigner wearing〔with〕a yellow hat？　3. Excuse me, could you tell me the way to the Taipei Railroad Station？　4. Are you in the habit of keeping a diary？　5. 他們常常趕夜工。　6. 她的錶已被偷走。　7. 警察把門推開。　8. 遊手好閒的人總是發現時間不易打發。

Test 3

1. 天氣一天比一天熱起來了。

---

2. 我不是告訴過你，我到車站的時候他們已經走了嗎？

---

3. 我最近胖了很多，所以許多衣服都穿不下了。

---

4. 「你們有舊車出售嗎？」
   「沒有。我們從來不經營舊車生意。」

---

5. Your voice will come in handy in case of fire.

---

6. My mother took me to task for not studying.

---

7. My cousin Tom will be of age next year.

---

8. He is a young man who shows promise.

【解答】

1. It〔The weather〕is getting hotter and hotter every day.   2. Didn't I tell you that they had gone by the time I got to the station？
3. I have gained much weight recently, so a lot of my clothes do not fit me now.   4. "Do you have any used car(s) for sale？" "No, we never deal in used cars."   5. 如果火警的話，你的嗓子就派得上用場了。   6. 我媽媽因為我不用功唸書而責備我。   7. 我的表哥湯姆明年成年。   8. 他是個有前途的年輕人。

Test 4

1. 一般人都知道閱讀對孩子有益。

2. 當他遭遇困難的時候，他根本不把它們放在眼裏。

3. 別忘記一定要在文件上簽你的名字。

4. 它遠不及以前漂亮。

5. The ideas which have always filled me with the joy of living are goodness, beauty, and truth.

6. I am convinced of the value of keeping a diary.

7. I have no say in this matter, (*and*) so I can't put in a word for him.

8. She began to take her husband for granted until he threatened to leave her.

【解答】

1. People know that reading is beneficial for children.
2. When he met with difficulties, he made nothing of them at all.
3. Be sure to put your signature to the document before you forget it.
4. It is not nearly so pretty as it was before.
5. 經常使我充滿生之喜悅的想法就是善、美、眞。   6. 我深信寫日記的價值。
7. 我無權過問此事，故無法爲他美言幾句。   8. 她開始是不在乎的樣子，直到她丈夫聲稱要離家出走，她才改變態度。

Test 5

1. 我們等不到半小時，霧便散了。

   _____

2. 約翰的批評毫無意義。

   _____

3. 謠傳她年輕時很漂亮。

   _____

4. 他口無遮攔。

   _____

5. People are bound to rub us the wrong way occasionally.

   _____

6. Don't you ever say that again.

   _____

7. Dr. Sun was a statesman, if ever there was one in China.

   _____

8. She distrusts me, and vice versa.

   _____

【解答】

1. We hadn't waited half an hour when the fog lifted.　2. John's criticism amounts to nothing.　3. Rumor has it that she was very beautiful when young.　4. He has got a loose tongue.　5. 人們有時必然會冒犯我們
6. 不許你再這麼說了。　7. 中國若無政治家則已，若有即孫博士是也。
8. 她不信任我，反之亦然。

Test 6

1. 戰爭之爆發是他們生活中的轉捩點。

_____

2. 沒有人不愛自己的國家。

_____

3. 他們當中即使有也很少人在這場大火災過後活下來。

_____

4. 的確，這個錶很貴，可是卻很值得。

_____

5. The snow began to come down and in earnest.

_____

6. He is more than pleased with this result.

_____

7. He is poor as much so or more so as I.

_____

8. Whenever there is a quarrel, there he is sure to be.

_____

【解答】

　　1. The outbreak of war was the turning point in their life.　　2. There is no one who doesn't love his own country.　　3. Very few of them, if any, survived the great fire.　　4. This watch is expensive, to be sure, but it is worthy of the price.　　5. 開始下雪了，而且下得很大。　　6. 他對這結果非常滿意。　　7. 他像我一樣窮，或許更窮。　　8. 無論何處有口角，他一定在場。

Test 7

1. 敬人者，人恒敬之。

_____

2. 她似乎認為讀書沒有什麼重要。

_____

3. 這張相片越看越不像你。

_____

4. 到下個月，我在台北就住了 10 年了。

_____

5. No work is low as long as it is honest.

_____

6. Always pick up your own litter after a picnic.

_____

7. So long as one does not look upon life bitterly, things work
out fairly well in the end.

_____

8. Your father shall hear of this.

_____

【解答】

1. Those who respect others will be (or _are_) constantly respected (_by others_).　2. She seems to think nothing of studying.　3. The more I look at the photograph, the less it looks like you.　4. I shall have lived in Taipei for 10 years by next month.　5. 工作只要正當，沒有貴賤之分。　6. 每次郊遊後，一定要把自己的垃圾撿起來。　7. 一個人只要不把生活看得很痛苦，事情到最後會解決得相當好。　8. 我一定要把此事告訴你父親。

Test 8

1. 我有他二倍多的參考書。

2. 多賴科學，我們如今過著比我們祖先更好的生活。

3. 模仿是猴子的特性。

4. 萬一失敗我們怎麼辦？

5. His honesty leaves no room for doubt.

6. She sings well as amateur singers go.

7. Don't give up because it is difficult.

8. The new arrival was none other than our lady principal.

【解答】

1. I have more than double the amount of reference books that he has.
2. Thanks to science, we now live〔lead〕a better life〔existence〕than our ancestors.　3. Imitation is a characteristic of monkeys.
4. What if we should fail？　5. 他的誠實不容懷疑。　6. 就一個業餘歌手來說，她算是唱得好的。　7. 不要因為困難而畏縮退卻。　8. 剛到的人不外乎我們女校長本人。

Test 9

1. 他繼承了父親的衣缽而當了律師。

_____

2. 他愈加耗費精力是不值得的。

_____

3. 商人把信歸檔。

_____

4. 他善於掩飾自己的無知。

_____

5. To her horror, she saw clouds of smoke issuing from her house.

_____

6. Let's agree to disagree and part friends.

_____

7. He stimulated areas in a patient's brain within a region as large as a match head.

_____

8. It might seem forward of me to think I could protect her.

_____

【解答】

1. He followed in his father's footsteps and became a doctor.　2. It does not pay to burn the candle at both ends.　3. Business people keep their letters on file.　4. He is clever at covering up his own ignorance.　5. 令她恐慌的是，她看到一陣煙從她的房子冒出來。　6. 讓我們包容彼此不同的意見而友善地分手吧。　7. 他把病人的腦中像火柴頭般大小的地方加以刺激。　8. 我似乎太大膽，認為我能保護她。

Test 10

1. 所有的同學都停下筆來注視我。

_____

2. 我不敢確定地說他將於何時到達。

_____

3. 你能肯定他從不說謊嗎？

_____

4. 無人知道何以一提到她的名字，Dick 就大為發怒。

_____

5. That there is a natural difference between virtue and vice, no reasonable man will deny.

_____

6. The true sportsman shows the greater pluck the more the odds are against him.

_____

7. As far as traffic safety is concerned, most drivers in Taipei should be re-educated.

_____

8. He is far too wise a man not to see that.

_____

_____

【解答】

　　1. All the classmates stopped writing to look at me.　2. I cannot say with certainty when he will arrive.　3. Are you sure he never lies?

　　4. Nobody knew why Dick flew into a rage at the mention of her name.

　　5. 在美德與罪惡之間自然有其不同之處，這是任何明理的人都不會否認的。

　　6. 真正的運動員，困難越多，越有勇氣。　7. 就交通安全而言，台北的駕駛員大部分應該再教育。　8. 他是聰明人，不會看不出那一點。

Test 11

1. 眞愛最顯著的特徵是對被愛者福祉積極的關切。

_____

2. 人類之不同於禽獸，是在於人類能夠思想和說話。

_____

3. 商人隨著探險者而來。

_____

4. 我因晚了兩分鐘而沒有趕上火車。

_____

5. We have been at sixes and sevens since the manager left.

_____

6. Fools don't become less foolish when they grow old.

_____

7. If she has a good voice, she's going to set the world on fire one day.

_____

8. He turned a deaf ear to what I said.

_____

【解答】

1. The most striking characteristic of true love is the active concern for the welfare of the loved.　　2. Men are different from brutes in their ability to think and to speak.　　3. Traders came in the wake of the explorers.　　4. I missed the train by two minutes.　　5. 經理走了我們就亂七八糟。　　6. 傻子到老還是傻子。　　7. 如果她有一付好嗓子，有一天她會成名的。　　8. 他對我的話充耳不聞。

Test 12

1. 健康是財富最不可能買到的東西。

___

2. 咱們一面喝酒一面討論吧。

___

3. 到目前爲止，他獻身教育工作已二十多年了。

___

4. 你所需要的是躺下來休息一會兒。

___

5. She never departs from her word.

___

6. Compassion is foreign to a selfish man.

___

7. Grandfather is too ill to need a doctor.

___

8. All at once I grew frightened and ran away.

___

【解答】

1. Health is the last thing that wealth can buy.　2. Let's discuss it over wine.　3. Up to the present, he has devoted himself to educational work for more than twenty years.　4. What you have to do is lie down and rest for a while.　5. 她從不食言。　6. 同情心是決不發生在一個自私的人身上的。　7. 祖父病得太厲害，請醫生來也沒有用。　8. 我忽然害怕起來跑走了。

Test 13

1. 收集了這麼多郵票，費了你多久的時間？

_____

2. 他買了一束玫瑰花給他太太。

_____

3. 讀書之於心靈，正如運動之於身體。

_____

4. 直到半夜，他才上床睡覺。

_____

5. I like to swim in fresh water.

_____

6. All the female audience enjoyed passing for young ladies.

_____

7. He has a palace of a house.

_____

8. After the long winter, spring was a mixed blessing, for it often rained.

_____

【解答】

1. How long did it take you to collect so many stamps ?　2. He bought a bunch (bouquet) of roses for his wife.　3. As exercise is to the body, so is reading to the mind.　4. He did not go to bed until midnight.　5. 我喜歡在淡水游泳。　6. 所有女聽衆都喜歡被看成是年輕女士。
7. 他有一棟像宮殿般的房子。　8. 漫長的冬天過後，春天是好壞參半，因爲時常下雨。

Test 14

1. 美國男孩跟女孩約會時，他們總是各付各的帳。

_____

2. 世界上沒有比人的生命更尊貴的東西。

_____

3. 因為沒有計程車，我們只好走路。

_____

4. 他驚訝得說不出話來。

_____

5. She often says that she's been under the weather of late.

_____

6. $ 300 is not nearly enough for the trip.

_____

7. Your friend is no better than a robber.

_____

8. Some people say that honesty does not pay, but I don't think it is true.

_____

【解答】

1. When an American boy dates a girl, they always go Dutch.　2. Nothing in the world is more valuable than human life.　3. There being no taxis, we had to walk.　4. Astonishment deprived him of his power of speech.　5. 她常說她最近感到身體不適。　6. 三百元根本不夠這趟旅行之用。
7. 你的朋友簡直就像強盜。　8. 有人說誠實不划算，但我卻不認為真是如此。

Test 15

1. 他怎樣生活的，我簡直猜不透。

2. 希望我們的壘球隊在比賽中得到冠軍。

3. 第二天是出乎意料的好天氣，最適合旅行。

4. 我一開始想買汽車，但是後來改變主意了。

5. Don't count your chickens before they are hatched.

6. It doesn't pay to walk such a long distance to buy a book.

7. The young traveler bounded forward, as if his feet had suddenly been endowed with the power of wings.

8. Miss Sarah was a kind woman for all her rude manners.

【解答】

1. How he keeps going is more than I can tell.　2. We hope that our softball team will win the championship.　3. The following day was unexpectedly fine, and it was most favorable for traveling.　4. I wanted to buy a car at first, but thought better of it afterwards. 5. 不要在蛋尚未孵出時先數難。（勿過分指望沒把握的事。）　6. 爲了買一本書而跑這麼遠的路程划不來。　7. 這年輕旅客向前躍去，他的雙腳像突然插了雙翅會飛似的。　8. 撒拉小姐是個仁慈的婦女，雖然她的態度無禮。

Test 16

1. 現在該是你們停止爭吵的時候了。

_____

2. 二十歲以上的人，佔全部人口的百分之三十。

_____

3. 你沒有給我選擇的餘地。

_____

4. 他答應要徹底遵守這個合約。

_____

5. The salesgirl gave me a twenty percent discount.

_____

6. The late professor Wang was a well-known physicist.

_____

7. It was not long before he came.

_____

8. You are no more a lady than I am a gentleman.

_____

【解答】

1. It's time that you put an end to your quarreling.　2. People over twenty years of age make up 30% of the total population.　3. You leave me no choice.　4. He promised to follow the contract to the letter.　5. 女店員給我打八折。　6. 已故的王教授是一位著名的物理學家。
7. 他不久就來了。　8. 妳不是個淑女，我也不會是個紳士。

Test 17

1. 洗衣機是用來洗衣服的。

---

2. 他有背名詩的癖好。

---

3. 我本希望不給他看見的。

---

4. 貧而無諂，不如富而好禮。

---

5. The human story does not always unfold like a mathematical calculation on the principle that two and two make four.

---

6. A sportsman has no patience with the man who plays at playing.

---

7. The lucky are not always on a highway to success; nor are the unlucky doomed to fail.

---

8. Given encouragement and help, he would not have failed.

【解答】

1. A washing machine is used to wash clothes.　2. He has a passion for committing famous poems to memory.　3. I wished I had not been seen by her.　4. One would rather be rich and courteous than poor, though unfawning.　5. 人類的故事未必像數學的計算一樣，依照二加二等於四的原則發展。　6. 運動員無法容忍在比賽時不認眞的人。　7. 幸運者未必永遠成功；不幸的人未必註定永遠失敗。　8. 假如他曾經受到鼓勵和幫助，就不會失敗了。

Test 18

1. 正因為她天眞坦率，我更加喜歡她。

   _____

2. 不是我不愛他，而是我對他期望過高。

   _____

3. 他目前和他的姑媽住在一起。

   _____

4. 他是那種喜歡挑別人毛病的人。

   _____

5. Clare knocked herself out preparing a delicious supper for her guests.

   _____

6. The suspect confessed that he had something to do with the murder case.

   _____

7. If he persists in laziness, he might as well withdraw from school.

   _____

8. The wind blows south.

   _____

【解答】

1. I like her all the better for her innocence.　2. Not that I don't like him, but that I expect too much of him.　3. He is living with his aunt for the time being.　4. He's the kind of person who likes to find fault with others.　5. 克蕾竭力為她的來賓準備美味的晚餐。
6. 疑犯供認他跟兇殺案有關係。　7. 如果他持續懈怠下去，倒不如退學算了。
8. 風從南邊吹來。

Test 19

1. 難怪我發現抽屜是開的。

2. 我喜歡拍鳥類和昆蟲的照片。

3. 那駕車人眞好，免費載我。

4. 他是你最好的朋友，再怎麼說也不會出賣你。

5. You ought to have the grass cut.

6. A strong determination will make light of difficulties.

7. I could give you a forty percent discount on this merchandise.

8. I cannot and will not accept your proposal.

【解答】

1. It's not surprising I found the drawer open.　2. I like to take pictures of birds and insects.　3. The motorist was so kind as to give me a lift(ride).
4. As your best friend, he will be the last person to betray you.
5. 你該找人來割草。　6. 堅強的決心將減輕（克服）困難。　7. 這種商品我可以給你打六折。　8. 我不能也不願接受你的建議。

Test 20

1. 今早，我死裏逃生！一部大卡車差點撞到我。

_____

2. 現在使用的清潔劑，卻有一些非常驚人的結果。

_____

3. 倘若林先生不能去台北開會，我可以代替他。

_____

4. 無論何事，盡力而為。

_____

5. Having worked twelve hours, I am good and tired.

_____

6. The way our drivers drive, we cannot be too careful when crossing the streets.

_____

7. I once took up the cudgels for Spingarn.

_____

8. Both of them are not happy.

_____

【解答】

1. I had a close call！A big car almost hit me this morning.　2. The detergents that are now in use, however, have some very surprising results.　3. If Mr. Lin cannot go to Taipei to attend the conference, I'll go instead.　4. Be the matter what it may, do your best.　5. 工作了十二小時，我非常累。　6. 我們的司機們那種開車的方式，使我們過街的時候愈小心愈好（再怎麼小心也不為過）。　7. 我一度很熱烈地支持史賓格。　8. 並不是他們兩人都快樂。

Test 21

1. 不久我們便到達車站了。

_____

2. 寬恕別人與被人寬恕同蒙其利。

_____

3. 我恐怕他會反對我們的計劃。

_____

4. 假如你當時把小包用掛號寄出,便不會在途中下落不明。

_____

5. A strong national defense is the most certain guarantee of peace and freedom.

_____

6. He knows better than to tell the truth to her.

_____

7. Hard work, unless balanced by relaxation of mind and body, may eventually destroy you.

_____

8. People consume more time in moving about than they did.

_____

【解答】

1. It was not long before we got to the station. 2. It is as beneficial to forgive as to be forgiven. 3. I am afraid he might oppose our plan. 4. If you had had the parcel registered, it would not have been lost on the way. 5. 強大的國防是和平與自由最明確的保證。 6. 他決不致於傻到去告訴她真相。 7. 除非身心得到適度的調劑,否則辛勞的工作可能終將毀了你。 8. 人們到處走動,所耗的時間比從前更多。

Test 22

1. 今年夏天異乎尋常的悶熱乾燥。

   _____

2. 我希望將來能成爲攝影家。

   _____

3. 幸福的藝術，像繪畫的藝術一樣，愈早學習愈好。

   _____

4. 對別人有禮貌是不會吃虧的。

   _____

5. The day gains on the night.

   _____

6. She has been saying unpleasant things about me for some
   time, so today I'm going to have it out with her.

   _____

7. She is anything but a student.

   _____

8. We knew nothing about the American-Japan policy.

   _____

   _____

【解答】

1. It is an unusually hot and dry summer this year. 2. I hope to be a photographer in the future. 3. The art of happiness, like that of painting, should be learned as early as possible. 4. It will do nobody harm to be polite to others. 5. 白天愈來愈長，晚上愈來愈短。 6. 她說了我一陣壞話，所以今天我要跟她好好談判。 7. 她決不是一個學生。 8. 有關美國的對日政策，我們毫不知情。

Test 23

1. 綁架幼童應處死刑。

2. "我可以打開窗子嗎？" "哦！可以，請吧！"

3. 這是千載難逢的機會。

4. 他們開懷暢飲。

5. I decided to go to the house of a friend who always kept late hours.

6. It was not until after World War II that man knew the importance of nuclear energy.

7. You should always put a little money aside for a rainy day.

8. He is making money hand over fist.

【解答】

1. Kidnapping of children should be punishable by death.
2. "Would you mind my opening the window?" "Oh, no; please do."
3. It was now or never.　　4. They drink to their heart's content.
5. 我決定到一位總是晚睡的朋友的家裡。　　6. 第二次世界大戰後，人類才知道核能的重要。　　7. 你該經常預備點錢，以備不時之需。　　8. 他正穩定而迅速地賺錢。

Test 24

1. 我不會飛，也不會游泳。

_____

2. 那些外國人不久就習慣於此地的氣候了。

_____

3. 阿里山的空氣也很新鮮，是台北所没有的。

_____

4. 叫他早點來。

_____

5. I had no comment to make on his criticism of the program.

_____

6. I knew what this money was for ; it was to get me started on my own.

_____

7. Rumors of an impending transit strike proved to be a false alarm.

_____

8. My father is a very well-known man of letters.

_____

_____

【解答】

1. I cannot swim any more than I can fly.　2. The foreigners soon became accustomed to the climate here.　3. The air on Mount Ali is quite fresh, too, which cannot be found in Taipei.　4. Let him come early.
5. 有關他對此節目的評論，我不予置評。　6. 我知道這筆錢的用途是要幫我自立。
7. 有關交通罷工的傳說，原來是一場虛驚。　8. 我父親是位很有名的文學家。

Test 25

1. 他的作爲帶有唱反調的味道。

2. 這整件事我將撒手不管了。

3. 不用說，他將信守諾言。

4. 昨天早上我出門的時候，天氣相當暖和。

5. Where there is a will, there is a way.

6. Oh, boy! Can't you just mind your own business?

7. Our members include people from all walks of life.

8. He affected not to have any interest in it.

【解答】

1. His doings smack of contradiction.　2. I am going to wash my hands of the whole thing.　3. It goes without saying that he will abide by his promise.　4. When I left home yesterday morning, the weather was quite warm.　5. 有志者事竟成。　6. 啊，老天！你不能只管你自己的事嗎？
7. 我們的會員包括各行各業的人。　8. 他假裝對它不感興趣。

Test 26

1. 說來話長。

___

2. 這條鐵路延長到國境。

___

3. 爲提供一個無煙的用餐環境，許多餐廳不允許室內抽煙。

___

4. 我從不曾一見鍾情。

___

5. He forgot the judge in the father.

___

6. They sometimes caused serious side effects.

___

7. A man would rather have some skill in a certain profession
than be a Jack of all trades.

___

8. My teacher took me to task for neglecting my lessons.

___

【解答】

1. It is a long story.　2. This railroad extends as far as the frontier.
3. To provide a nonsmoking dining environment, many restaurants don't
allow smoking indoors.　4. I have never loved at first sight.
5. 他在充滿父愛之下忘記了法官的冷靜和職責。
6. 它們有時會引起嚴重的副作用。　7. 與其博而不精，不如一技在身。
8. 我的老師責備我疏忽功課。

Test 27

1. 我們常在夏天到那裏游泳、釣魚。

_____

2. 如果能常常到山上去,那是多麼好啊!

_____

3. 她經常飯前洗手。

_____

4. 你介意我打開收音機嗎?

_____

5. There is something intellectual about the girl.

_____

6. That's my proposal. Take it or leave it.

_____

7. I love him all the better for his faults.

_____

8. I can't bring myself to tell her the news.

_____

【解答】

1. We would often swim and fish there during the summer.　2. How I wish I could often go to the mountain.　3. She makes it a rule to wash her hands before meals.　4. Do you mind if I turn on the radio? 5. 這女孩頗有聰明之處。　6. 那是我的建議,要不要隨你。　7. 就是因為他的缺點,我更愛他。　8. 我鼓不起勇氣告訴她這個消息。

Test 28

1. 運動對健康有益。

2. 一個人最珍視什麼樣的感情，他就會成為什麼樣的人。

3. 他在砍樹時跌倒了。

4. 當我問他該事對他是否很重要，他說一點也不重要。

5. He came of a line of people who knew a spade when they saw one.

6. You do have something up your sleeve. Come out with it.

7. Don't permit your youth to become slaves to material goods, until finally they will prefer slavery to the struggle for freedom.

8. Don't review past failures, guessing endlessly what might have been.

【解答】

1. Exercise is good for health. 2. A man will be what his most cherished feelings are. 3. He fell down when he was felling a tree. 4. When I asked him whether it was of any account to him, he said it did not matter a bit. 5. 他出身於世代務農之家。 6. 你確實胸有成竹。說來聽聽吧。 7. 不要使你們的青年貪圖物質享受，終至於甘願做敵人的奴隸，而不願做自由的鬥士。 8. 切勿回顧過去的失敗，而且一直不斷地猜想可能會如何。

Test 29

1. 考完試後我要好好的休息。

_____

2. 犯過的人該受處罰。

_____

3. 在去世以前，他一直不停地寫詩。

_____

4. 在她十歲以前，海倫已經是全國性的人物。

_____

5. He earns scarcely enough to keep body and soul together.

_____

6. The baseball players went all out to win the game.

_____

7. I have everything I want. I'm on top of the world now.

_____

8. Twenty dollars a week doesn't go far.

_____

【解答】

1. I want to have a good rest after the test.　2. Those who do wrong
deserve punishing.　3. He had been writing poems ceaselessly until he
died.　4. Before she was ten years old, Helen had become a national
figure.　5. 他所賺的錢難以糊口。　6. 爲了贏得比賽，棒球選手們全力以赴。
7. 我想要的我都有了。我現在眞是稱心如意。　8. 一星期二十元無濟於事。

Test 30

1. 你到底怎麼搞的？

2. 放心吧！你儘管走好了。

3. 他們在一小時以前就應該已經會面了。

4. 我生長在鄉下的一個小村落。

5. Of two evils, choose the lesser.

6. Your joke is worth repeating.

7. The robbers who robbed the bank are still at large.

8. I got a good deal on this microwave oven.

【解答】

1. What in the world is the matter with you?　2. You may just as well go. Don't worry !　3. They should have met an hour ago.　4. I grew up in a small village in the country.　5. 兩權相害取其輕。　6. 你的笑話值得回味。　7. 那些搶銀行的強盜仍然未被逮捕。　8. 我買這個微波烤箱買得很便宜。

Test 31

1. 就像其他合成的產品一樣，這些清潔劑不會分解。

2. 經常的示威使台北的交通問題更形惡化。

3. 這張相片使我想起童年。

4. 不要和幫派少年交朋友，他們會帶你走入歧途。

5. No other country accepted the proposal, much less acted upon it.

6. A white dress to wear with a red tie would really fix you up.

7. I am sure that Mr. Brown will be home by and by.

8. Perseverance is what makes people succeed.

【解答】
1. Like other synthetic products, these detergents will not dissolve. 2. Frequent demonstrations have aggravated Taipei's traffic problems. 3. The picture reminds me of my childhood. 4. Don't keep company with gangsters who will lead you astray. 5. 沒有其他國家接受這提議，更沒有採取行動的。 6. 白衣服配上紅領帶實在很配稱。 7. 我確信布朗先生不久就會回家。 8. 堅毅使人成功。

Test 32

1. 鉛筆該削了。

2. 學問無止境。

3. 他為什麼老是上課遲到？

4. 這個月，我的運氣眞是好得我都不敢相信。

5. He is above suspicion.

6. Because there are not enough chairs to go around, some people have to stand.

7. John caught cold last night, and now he aches all over.

8. Many people strive for things other than money and fame.

【解答】

1. The pencil needs sharpening.　2. There is no royal road to learning.
3. How come it is that he is always late for class?　4. I can hardly believe (that) I have been so lucky this month.　5. 他無可懷疑。
6. 因爲椅子不夠分配，有些人不得不站著。　7. 約翰昨晚著了涼，現在他渾身酸痛。　8. 許多人所努力追求的是名利以外之物。

Test 33

1. 人們使用肥皂好幾百年了，並沒有破壞環境。

_____

2. 待人誠實是不吃虧的。

_____

3. 人有時候會無意之間表露出眞情。

_____

4. 經過多年，我老師的忠告仍留在我耳際。

_____

5. He is very particular about his food.

_____

6. We shouldn't be indifferent to the sufferings of others.

_____

7. When the naughty boy broke the window again, his father hit the ceiling.

_____

8. The school tennis champion was too much for me.

_____

【解答】

1. People have used soap for hundreds of years but have not spoiled the environment. 2. It pays to be honest to others. 3. Once in a while one may unknowingly show one's true feelings. 4. After many years my teacher's advice still rings in my ears. 5. 他對食物很講究。 6. 我們不該對別人的痛苦漠不關心。 7. 當那頑皮的男孩又打破窗戶時，他老爹勃然大怒。 8. 這位學校的網球冠軍非我所能敵。

Test 34

1. 水由氫氧構成。

_____

2. 我會設法克制我的脾氣，而且不再對我的妹妹大吼大叫。

_____

3. 他因生性慷慨而花了一千元。

_____

4. 天曉得他下次會說些什麼。

_____

5. Time soothes all sorrows.

_____

6. You have to admit that his words amount to nothing.

_____

7. She sells stories to keep the wolf from the door.

_____

8. Speaking the language the way you do, you can pass for a native.

_____

【解答】

1. Water is made up of hydrogen and oxygen.　2. I'll try to control my temper and not shout at my sister any more.　3. His generosity cost him one thousand dollars.　4. Heaven knows what he'll say next.

5. 時間可減輕哀傷。　6. 你得承認他的話毫無意義。　7. 她投稿爲了糊口。

8. 聽你講話，別人會認爲你是當地人。

Test 35

1. 我的脚踏車上禮拜天被偷了。

_____

2. 聽衆對那演講者發噓聲，因他說話不得要領。

_____

3. 天黑前很可能會下雨，不過半小時內大概不會下。

_____

4. 他買了三本書，其中一本是詩集。

_____

5. Something must be done about Taipei's traffic before it paralyzes the city.

_____

6. It takes nerve to be cheerful when one is in a predicament.

_____

7. Take time before time takes you.

_____

8. In a matter of minutes, information and ideas can be exchanged with people living all over the world.

_____

【解答】

1. I had my bicycle stolen last Sunday.　　2. The audience hissed at the speaker, who did not speak to the point.　　3. It's possible to rain before dark, but not probable in half an hour.　　4. He bought three books, one of which is a collection of poems.　　5. 在交通癱瘓整個台北市之前，我們必須有所改革。　　6. 苦中作樂需有勇氣。　　7. 在死以前，好好把握住時間。　　8. 大約幾分鐘的時間，居住在世界各地的人們可以互相交換資料和構想。

Test 36

1. 我們在那邊所看到的屋頂是什麼建築物的屋頂？

2. 我直到清晨兩點才就寢。

3. 當你與別人爭論時，務必保持冷靜。

4. 我的法國客人尚不慣於用筷子。

5. He never goes to a bookstore without buying some books.

6. A good beginning is half of success.

7. That company was in the red last year.

8. More is meant than meets the ear.

【解答】

　1. What is that building whose roof we see over there？　　2. I didn't go to bed until two o'clock in the morning.　　3. Keep your head while you are arguing with others.　　4. My French guest is not yet used to using chopsticks.　　5. 他每次進書店，一定買一些書。　　6. 好的開始是成功的一半。　　7. 那家公司去年是赤字（虧損）。　　8. 言外有意。

Test 37

1. 老實說，一直到昨天我才知道他已經去美國了。

---

2. 李小姐怕胖而節食。

---

3. 中正紀念堂的莊嚴壯麗非言語所能形容。

---

4. 人為萬物之靈。

---

5. It never rains but it pours.

---

6. As far as the problem of violence on television is concerned, I don't see eye to eye with you.

---

7. It's the last thing I feel like doing.

---

8. You may pick whatever takes your fancy.

【解答】

1. To be frank, not until yesterday did I know that he had gone to the United States.　2. Miss Lee is dieting because she's afraid of putting on weight.

3. The solemness and magnificence of Chiang Kai-Shek's Memorial Hall is beyond discription.　4. Man is the lord of creation.　5. 不雨則已；一雨傾盆。（喻禍不單行。）　6. 對於電視上暴力的問題，我和你的看法不同。

7. 這是我絕不想要做的事。　8. 你喜歡什麼就挑什麼。

Test 38

1. 他所說的話無可否認。

2. 她的嫻靜和職業上的能幹都同樣令人懷念。

3. 永遠要對自己的行爲負責。

4. 我們和美國學生同樣地勤勉。

5. He sat reading and fell asleep without knowing it.

6. Anger is only one letter short of danger.

7. " Perseverance is what makes people succeed. "
   " I couldn't agree more. "

8. I will make a special point of seeing you before I leave
   for Taipei.

【解答】

1. There is no denying what he says.   2. She is remembered for her quiet charm as much as for her professional competence.   3. Always be in charge of your action.   4. We are no less diligent than American students.   5. 他坐著讀書，不知不覺睡著了。   6. 一發怒就接近危險。
7. "堅毅使人成功。""我十分贊成。"   8. 去台北前我一定會先來看看你。

Test 39

1. 台灣的人口已超過兩千萬。

_____

2. 她昨天不告而別。

_____

3. 我未曾聽過別人說她的壞話。

_____

4. 不論晴雨,該比賽將於下星期一上午舉行。

_____

5. He has never failed other people's trust.

_____

6. The member countries were asked to step up their production.

_____

7. There is no saying what he'll be doing next.

_____

8. Babbit was the only professor who was only an M. A. by degree in the university.

_____

【解答】

1. The population of Taiwan has exceeded twenty million.　2. She took French leave yesterday.　3. I have never heard her spoken ill of.
4. Rain or shine, the tournament will be held next Monday morning.
5. 他從未辜負旁人的信賴。　6. 會員國被要求增加其產量。　7. 不知道他下次要做什麼。　8. 貝比特是這所大學的教授中,唯一只有碩士學位的人。

Test 40

1. 我的錶停了，一定忘記上絃了。

2. 當宴會結束時，他堅持要送她回家。

3. 你們聰明有餘，用功不足。

4. 大多數的學生都不曉得如何使用圖書館。

5. We all want to be looked up to.

6. Can you make over this dress?

7. At that, the young man took his departure on the fly.

8. The result was nothing short of my expectation.

【解答】

1. My watch had left off. I must have forgotten to wind it up.　2. When the party was over, he made it a point to see her home.　3. You are more wise than diligent.　4. Most students do not know how to use a library.　5. 我們都希望被尊敬。　6. 你能修改這件衣服嗎？　7. 聽到那件事，那個年輕人就匆忙地離開了。　8. 那結果正如我所預料。

Test 41

1. 在那兒抽煙的人是我爸爸。

2. 前幾天，英語演講比賽我得了第二名。

3. 我們一直在為春假旅行做計畫。

4. 站住！

5. There is no parking lot, so we'd better not park our car here, or we will be fined.

6. You have to admit that what he says makes perfect sense.

7. She took over the business after her husband died.

8. It's not easy to fool him; he's been around.

【解答】

1. The person smoking over there is my father.　2. A few days ago, I won second place in the English speech contest.　3. We have been making plans for the spring vacation.　4. Stay where you are!

5. 沒有停車場，所以我們最好不要把車停在這裡，不然會被罰款。　6. 你得承認他的話很有道理。　7. 她先生死後，她接管了他的事業。　8. 戲弄他不容易，因為他經驗豐富。

Test 42

1. 不久的將來我們就可再見面。

2. 自從我來台灣以後，到過不少地方去旅行。

3. 他雖有缺點，然而我們一樣尊敬他。

4. 耐心再好，總不會永無止境。

5. A man sits as many risks as he runs.

6. He tried to get the most of each dollar he spent.

7. I don't quite enjoy his company.

8. What a weird fellow he is！ I can't make him out at all.

【解答】

1. It won't be long before we meet again.　2. I have traveled to many places (ever) since I came to Taiwan.　3. He has faults, but we respect him none the less.　4. There is always a limit to one's patience.　5. 做事有險，不做事也有險。　6. 他設法好好利用他花去的每一塊錢。　7. 我不太喜歡和他在一起。　8. 他真是個怪人！我一點也不能了解他。

Test 43

1. 這輩子，我的運氣從來沒有這麼好過。

_____

2. 我的同學大多數很欣賞我的照片。

_____

3. 小心扒手。

_____

4. 對我的提議他充耳不聞。

_____

5. There was no dissuading him from doing so.

_____

6. The door opened of its own accord.

_____

7. John is no more a prominent musician than Mary is.

_____

8. There is a sample attached to the letter.

_____

_____

【解答】

1. So far in my life, I have never been so lucky. 2. Most of my classmates appreciate my pictures very much. 3. Beware of pick-pockets. 4. He turned a deaf ear to my proposition. 5. 不可能勸阻他這麼做。 6. 那扇門自動開了。 7. 約翰和瑪麗都不是傑出的音樂家。 8. 信中附有樣品。

Test 44

1. 不知道甚麼時候才能再見到童年的美景。

2. 在某些地區，水龍頭流出來的水很不好聞。

3. 直到每人表達了他的意見之後，我們才能做決定。

4. 除了音樂外，他最喜歡網球。

5. He begged to be remembered to you.

6. Facts and opinions are often at odds.

7. It was merely a false alarm.

8. Come, come. Let's not quarrel any more.

【解答】

　1. I don't know when I'll be able to see that beautiful sight of my childhood again.

　2. In some areas, the water running out of the tap smells bad.

　3. It is not until everyone expresses his opinion that we can make a decision.　　4. Besides music, he loves tennis best.　　5. 他要向你問安。

　6. 事實和意見往往相違背。　　7. 只是虛驚一場。　　8. 算了，算了。我們別再吵啦。

Test 45

1. 今日電腦已被廣泛運用於工業和國防上。

2. 眼鏡蛇盤在他脚下，他仍表現得若無其事。

3. 迄今我仍未接到他的信。

4. 抱歉，我幫不上忙。

5. He was shown into an office.

6. This law did more harm than good in that it made progress impossible.

7. Houses which fail to satisfy these minimum requirements are to be pulled down.

8. Their business has grown by leaps and bounds.

【解答】
1. Today computers are widely used in industry and national defense.
2. With the cobra coiling around his foot, he still behaved as if nothing were the matter. 3. So far I haven't heard from him. 4. Sorry, there is nothing I can do to help. 5. 別人請他進辦公室。 6. 這條法律的壞處比好處多，因為它阻礙了進步。 7. 凡是不符合最低要求的房子，一律拆除。 8. 他們的事業進展神速。

Test 46

1. 我剛到，他就非走不可。

---

2. 可怕的夢魘幾乎使我發狂。

---

3. 我在今天的報紙上看到一則很有趣的新聞。

---

4. 不管家多麼簡陋，家總是最好的地方。

---

5. Let us do this painful thing while the fit is on us.

---

6. When asked how he was getting along in his new job, Mr. Wilson answered that he was far from being optimistic about it.

---

7. There is a fine line between love and hate.

---

8. True worth often goes unrecognized.

【解答】

1. I had no sooner arrived than he had to go.　2. The horrible nightmare almost drove me mad.　3. I read an interesting item of news in today's paper.　4. Be it ever so humble, there is no place like home.
5. 趁著心血來潮的時候，讓我們做這件痛苦的事吧！　6. 當被問及他的新工作進展如何時，威爾遜先生回答說他對他的工作一點也不樂觀。　7. 愛恨難分。
8. 眞正的價值經常不被認定。

Test 47

1. 假如約翰不能參加會議，我就代他去。

---

2. 各階層（各行各業）的人都喜歡看電視。

---

3. 告訴孩子們，他們如果不守規矩，就得不到禮物。

---

4. 假如你再犯相同的錯誤，你將被學校開除。

---

5. That incident made his hair stand on end.

---

6. So far I haven't heard from him yet.

---

7. He is anything but an artist.

---

8. Gambling has brought about his ruin.

【解答】

1. If John cannot attend the conference, I'll go instead.　2. People from every walk of life enjoy watching television.　3. Tell the children to behave or they are not getting any presents.　4. Make the same mistake again, and you shall be expelled from school.　5. 那件事使他毛骨悚然。　6. 到目前爲止，我沒有收到他的信息。　7. 他絕不是個藝術家。　8. 賭博使他傾家蕩產。

Test 48

1. 從他的口音來判斷，他似乎是一個美國人。

2. 老師應該多鼓勵學生到圖書館借書。

3. 比這個更有趣的故事，我從來沒有聽說過。

4. 遠水救不了近火。

5. His face is suggestive of a monkey.

6. Familiarity breeds contempt.

7. To think of our meeting here.

8. She gave me a bright and amicable flash of her teeth.

【解答】

1. Judging from his accent, he seems to be an American.　2. Teachers should encourage their students to borrow books from the library.　3. I have never heard a more interesting story.　4. Water(from) afar cannot put out(a) near fire.　5. 看到他的臉就想到猴子。　6. 過度親密，易起侮慢之心。　7. 眞沒想到我們竟在此碰面。　8. 她給我一個明朗而友善的微笑。

Test 49

1. 他非常努力，結果卻考不及格。

_____

2. 我連著吃了五天藥，感冒還是沒有好。

_____

3. 他們默默苦幹。

_____

4. 消息很短，而且中肯。

_____

5. My guess could be anything but fair.

_____

6. The portrait is drawn to the life.

_____

7. Who has the say in the matter ?

_____

8. She said to me, " Nothing doing."

_____

_____

【解答】

1. He studied very hard, only to fail in the examination.   2. Although I have been taking medicine for five days on end, I haven't recovered from my cold yet.   3. They labored on in wordless silence.   4. The message is short and to the point.   5. 要我猜，一定猜不中。   6. 這幅像畫得維妙維肖。   7. 這件事誰有決定權？   8. 她對我說：「不行。」

Test 50

1. 目前明智之舉是忘卻你的憂慮。

_____

2. 你說他什麼時候會來？

_____

3. 他住在我們隔壁第二家。

_____

4. 你昨天打電話來的時候，我們正在吃午飯。

_____

5. " Do you think he is a cop?" " I think so."

_____

6. Conditions at present are on the mend.

_____

7. There's no way of knowing where the man came from, let alone identifying him by name.

_____

8. There is much to be desired in your work.

_____

【解答】

1. The sensible thing to do now is to put aside your worries.　2. When did you say he would come?　3. He lives next door to us but one.
4. We were having lunch when you called yesterday.　5.「你想他是位警察嗎？」「我想是吧。」　6. 目前情況好轉了。　7. 無法知曉他的來踪，更不必提他的名字了。　8. 你的工作有待改進。

Test 51

1. 我喜歡香蕉，更喜歡橘子。

---

2. 湯姆決心要在暑假中打零工，以完成他的大學學業。

---

3. 中東將不會有持久的和平。

---

4. 我會等你回心轉意。

---

5. I know he meant business.

---

6. Many drownings occur even in water of standing depth.

---

7. When a child, you must go by the wishes of your parents.

---

8. The man who follows the plough may be not so much in need of exercise as (*in need*) of recreation.

【解答】
1. I like bananas, but I like tangerines better. 2. Tom was determined to work his way through college (or *university*) by doing odd jobs during summer vacation. 3. There won't be lasting peace in the Middle East. 4. I will wait for you to change your mind. 5. 我知道他不是開玩笑的。 6. 甚至有很多溺斃的事件，都發生在水深只有一人高的地方。 7. 小孩子要聽父母的話。 8. 對做農事的人，與其說需要運動，不如說需要娛樂。

Test 52

1. 我的手錶雖便宜，卻準得很。

2. 她愈來愈令人難以忍受。

3. 我很少有旅行的時候不帶幾本書的。

4. 你曾經到過碧潭嗎？

5. She said she was through with singing.

6. His remarks hit home when he referred to the problem.

7. I could not help laughing; he looked so silly.

8. The smoke betrayed where the dwelling lay.

【解答】

1. Cheap as it is, my watch keeps good time. 2. My patience with her is wearing thin. 3. I seldom travel without taking some books with me. 4. Have you ever been to Green Lake? 5. 她說她不再唱歌了。 6. 當他提到那問題時，他的話一針見血。 7. 看他一付傻相，我禁不住笑了起來。 8. 炊煙起處有人家。

Test 53

1. 與其說她不擅社交，不如說她膽怯。

_____

2. 我們深受父母之恩。

_____

3. 月初，我的數學月考考了九十分。

_____

4. 中國人沒有守法的習慣。

_____

5. She has lost her tongue.

_____

6. I could make neither head nor tail out of that modern poem.

_____

7. Swimming brings into play all the muscles of the body.

_____

8. John's criticism amounts to nothing.

_____

【解答】

1. She is more shy than unsociable.　2. We owe a great deal to our parents.　3. Earlier this month, I got 90 points in the monthly math exam.　4. The Chinese do not have a habit of abiding by the law. 5. 她（因吃驚）說不出話來。　6. 我完全不懂那首現代詩。　7. 游泳使全身肌肉活動。　8. 約翰的批評毫無意義。

Test 54

1. 我想約翰已經走了，是嗎？

2. 春節期間，我曾經到過阿里山。

3. 我跟他的意見相同，就是讀書使人淵博。

4. 我認為這部車子不是他父親的。

5. The author is still in high popularity.

6. He is not above asking questions.

7. His bravery was beyond the call of duty.

8. My father's temper, which was at the mercy of his pride, was never to be trusted.

【解答】

1. I think John has left, hasn't he?　　2. During the Chinese New Year, I went to Mount Ali.　　3. I share his opinion that reading makes a full man.　　4. I don't think this car is his father's.　　5. 此作家仍然深受歡迎。　　6. 他不恥下問。　　7. 他的英勇遠超職責所求。　　8. 由於驕傲，我父親的脾氣令人捉摸不定。

Test 55

1. 在約定的時間他並未露面。

_____

2. 現在溪水髒得魚都不能活了。

_____

3. 任何人都不能單獨生存。

_____

4. 首先，我要說明清楚，我並不反對你的意見。

_____

5. When he woke up, the ship was at sea.

_____

6. The gratitude they felt could not be put into words.

_____

7. I would that we had more of it left.

_____

8. See to it that my instructions are followed to the letter.

_____

【解答】

1. He didn't show up at the appointed time.　　2. The stream is now so dirty that no fish can live there.　　3. No one can live alone.
4. First of all, I want to make it clear that I am not opposed to your idea.
5. 當他醒來時，船已在海上。　　6. 他們的感激難以言語表達。　　7. 我真希望我們多剩下一點。　　8. 務必徹底按照我交待的話去做。

Test 56

1. 我常常帶著我的老照相機到郊外去。

_____

2. 月中，父親送我一部電腦當生日禮物。

_____

3. 使我放心的是，他在幾分鐘後甦醒過來了。

_____

4. 你最好不要多管閒事。

_____

5. I went to a lecture on relativity but it was beyond my depth.

_____

6. I am sorry that I forgot myself. I was so carried away.

_____

7. They voiced their disapproval to a man.

_____

8. The rain lets up.

_____

【解答】

1. I often go to the suburbs with my old camera.　　2. In the middle of the month, my father gave me a computer as a birthday present.
3. To my relief, he came to himself in a few minutes.　　4. Hadn't you gone about your own business?　　5. 我去聽一場相對論的演講，但卻聽不懂。
6. 抱歉我失態了，我太感動了。　　7. 他們異口同聲一致反對。　　8. 雨停了。

Test 57

1. 他們的數學課程非常落伍。

_____

2. 我沒有跟陌生人開始談話的習慣。

_____

3. 似乎過了很久以後，叫做瑪雅（Maya）的女人才來接電話。

_____

4. 一分又一分鐘終於在滴嗒聲中過去了，他還是想不出答案來。

_____

5. It looks we are back to square one again.

_____

6. You'll not be drowned unless you are not prudent.

_____

7. He lives next door to us but one.

_____

8. Children are not so much to be taught as to be trained.

_____

【解答】

1. Their courses in mathematics are very outdated.　2. I am not in the habit of talking to strangers.　3. It seemed a long time before the woman called Maya answered the phone.　4. The minutes finally ticked away, and he still failed to come up with an answer.
5. 看起來我們又得從頭再來了。　6. 除非你不小心，不然不會淹死。　7. 他住在我們隔鄰第二家。　8. 兒童與其說是被教不如說是被訓練的。

Test 58

1. 雖然全世界都在讚美他，林白却保持清醒。

_____

2. 我過兩、三天再來看你。

_____

3. 工業使用電鍍的過程，首要是保護金屬表面，以免受到腐蝕。

_____

4. 油料快用光了。

_____

5. "Give and take" is a rule we must all go by.

_____

6. Medical men say swimming is the most perfect form of physical exercise, as it brings into play all the muscles of the body.

_____

7. In the case of iron, the refining process needs plenty of heat.

_____

8. I still cannot make out what he is driving at.

_____

【解答】

　　1. Though the whole world (or *all the world*) was praising him, Lindbergh kept his head.　　2. I'll come back to see you in a few days.　　3. Industry has used the process of electroplating first to protect metal surfaces lest they should corrode.　　4. The oil is running out.　　5.「互相謙讓」是我們都必須遵循的法則。　　6. 醫學家說游泳是最完美的身體運動方式，因爲游泳運用全身的肌肉。　　7. 就鐵而言，精錬過程需要高熱。　　8. 我仍不了解他的用意何在。

Test 59

1. 他繼續趕下去以彌補浪費掉的時間。

_____

2. 我們愈了解本國語言愈好。

_____

3. 那個人，知道了自己的過失，承認他拿了錢。

_____

4. 那時，我家附近有一條清澈的小溪。

_____

5. I'll be no party to you.

_____

6. What we need most is not so much to realize the ideal as to idealize the real.

_____

7. It takes rich imagination to be an inventor.

_____

8. Come what may, I'll stand for you.

_____

【解答】

1. He hurried on to make up for the lost time. 2. We can't know too much about our mother tongue. 3. The man, conscious of his fault, admitted having taken the money. 4. At that time, near our house was a clean stream. 5. 我不想與你來往。 6. 我們最需要的，與其說是實現理想，不如說把現實理想化。 7. 做一個發明家需要具備豐富的想像力。 8. 無論如何，我將支持你。

Test 60

1. 他最近常去打獵。

2. 現在大家都說他們無法相信我從前又矮又瘦。

3. 大家都喜歡好天氣。

4. 雖然功課一直很繁重，我還是每天慢跑半小時。

5. Had Betty known how deep I was in debt, she would not have taken French leave.

6. Her way of speaking rubbed her employer the wrong way.

7. He is said to have failed in the last examination.

8. He would probably do well in the examination, only that he gets rather nervous.

【解答】

　　1. He has done a lot of hunting recently.　　2. Now, people say that they cannot believe that I was once very small and thin.　　3. People like good weather.　　4. Even though my studies took up a great deal of my time, I continued to jog for half an hour every day.　　5. 要是蓓蒂知道我負債纍纍，她就不會不告而別。　　6. 她說話的方式激怒了她的雇主。　　7. 據說他上次考試不及格。　　8. 若不是他很緊張，他可能考得很好。

Test 61

1. 我們班有五十位學生（由五十位學生組成）。

_____

2. 以你的年齡而論，你是高的。

_____

3. 約有150個學生，在昨天考試時缺席。

_____

4. 我無論怎樣感謝我的老師也不爲過。

_____

5. There is no accounting for tastes.

6. In an examination, students are often hard put to find the right answers.

_____

7. Such talk is beneath us.

_____

8. She burst into tears; she couldn't help herself.

_____

【解答】

1. Our class is composed of fifty students.   2. You are tall for your age.
3. About 150 students were absent at yesterday's examination.
4. I cannot thank my teachers too much.   5. 人各有所好。   6. 考試的時候，學生往往很難找到正確的答案。   7. 講這種話未免有失我們的身分。   8. 她放聲大哭，她無法自制。

Test 62

1. 大體上說，他是不壞的。

2. 衆人之事無人管。

3. 讀小學的時候，我身體很虛弱，並且常感冒。

4. 我不知道它需要多久的時間。

5. The company was in the red last year.

6. Let's bring all these empty cans into play.

7. A wonderful reward is in store for him.

8. Something could have gone wrong.

【解答】

1. By and large, he is not bad.　2. Everybody's business is nobody's business.　3. When I was in elementary school, my body was very weak and I often caught colds.　4. I have no idea how long it will take.
5. 那家公司去年虧損。　6. 讓我們廢物利用。　7. 一份優厚的酬勞正在等待他。
8. 事情可能出差錯了。

Test 63

1. 自從上了國中以後，我就儘量找機會運動。

_____

2. 直到死後十年，這位作曲家才漸漸出名起來。

_____

3. 六年繼續不斷的鍛鍊使我不但更加強壯，而且也長得更高。

_____

4. 半因生病，半因虧損，他幾乎整個毀了。

_____

5. His help often turns out to be in my way.

_____

6. We owe our duty to our country.

_____

7. Old habits die hard.

_____

8. On what ground did you not come?

_____

【解答】

1. Beginning with junior high (school), I continuously looked for opportunities involving physical activity.　2. Not till a decade after his death did the composer gradually become noted (renown).　3. Six years of nonstop physical conditioning has made me not only stronger, but also taller.　4. What with illness and losses, he is almost ruined.　5. 他的幫助常常是愈幫愈忙。　6. 我們對國家負有義務。　7. 固習難改。　8. 你沒有來是何理由？

Test 64

1. 雖然遭到許多癮君子反對，這對不抽煙的人的確是一大福音。

2. 若不是他的鼓勵，我決不再試了。

3. 那位老電影明星據說年輕時是一位大美人。

4. 經常的示威使台北的交通問題更形惡化。

5. As I didn't have enough money, I bought the house on time.

6. Without frugality none can be rich, with it very few would be poor.

7. It is beyond my means to buy a new car.

8. I've never heard him spoken ill of.

【解答】

1. Although it is opposed by many smokers, it is indeed good news to nonsmokers.　2. But for his encouragement, I would not make any more attempt.　3. The old movie star is said to have been a beauty when she was young.　4. Constant demonstrations worsen the problem of traffic in Taipei.　5. 因為我沒有足夠的錢，我分期付款買房子。
6. 不儉則不富；節儉者必不長貧。　7. 買一部新車非我財力所及。
8. 我從未聽人說過他的壞話。

Test 65

1. 綁架幼童應處死刑。

_____

2. 我們不可能在十點鐘到達那裏。

_____

3. 他守口如瓶。

_____

4. 我什麼都肯做卻不願做那件事。

_____

5. Twenty failed, myself among the rest.

_____

6. It is not alore a proverb but a truth that a contented man is never unhappy.

_____

7. When we read an English book, we must not spare ourselves trouble to consult a dictionary constantly.

_____

8. People are beginning to realize the importance of their cultural heritage.

_____

【解答】

1. Those who kidnap little children should be sentenced to death.

2. It will be impossible for us to get there by ten o'clock.

3. His mouth is sealed.　　4. I would do anything but that.　　5. 二十位不及格（失敗了），我自己及格了。　　6. 知足常樂是格言，也是眞理。

7. 讀英文時，我們一定要勤查字典。　　8. 大家開始了解到他們自己的文化遺產的重要性。

Test 66

1. 你該不會在挖苦人吧？

2. 瑪麗長得很美，可是不夠高。

3. 考完試後我要好好的休息。

4. 今年夏天異乎尋常的悶熱乾燥。

5. How much should we pay for the down payment?

6. Sleeplessness will be responsible for many injuries.

7. The boy got panicky when the fire broke out.

8. Nothing lasts forever, but in the world of letters we find many enduring works.

【解答】

　　1. Do I detect a note of sarcasm in your voice?　2. Mary is beautiful, but she is not tall enough.　3. I want to take a good rest after the examination is over.　4. It seems to be extraordinarily hot and dry this summer.　5. 我們該付多少的頭款？　6. 失眠將導致許多害處。　7. 火警發生時，那男孩驚慌失措。　8. 沒有東西是永恆的，但在文學世界中，我們發現了許多不朽的作品。

Test 67

1. 為達到目的而不擇手段。

2. 你早該寫封短箋給王先生了。

3. 每天早晨有一位穿綠色制服的人，把信件送到我們的社區來。

4. 不要把今天該做的事拖延到明天。

5. Everybody was working against the clock.

6. When it comes to writing, he is nervous.

7. I hope to see more of you.

8. With regard to his eloquence, he is second to none.

【解答】

1. The end justifies the means.   2. It's time you wrote a note to Mr. Wang.   3. Every morning a man in a green uniform delivers letters to our community.   4. Don't put off until tomorrow what should be done today.   5. 大家為了趕時間，都拼命地幹活。   6. 一提到寫作他就緊張。
7. 我希望能常常見你。   8. 就辯才而言，他數第一。

Test 68

1. 台北的生活水準比大陸高多了。

2. 他的境況比三年前好得多。

3. 他不知該如何解決此問題。

4. 你最好還是早睡早起。

5. You should set an example for the future.

6. He denied himself ease and pleasure and worked hard.

7. Everything scared me in those days, and still does.

8. Call it what you like.

【解答】

　1. The living standard in Taipei is much higher than that on the Mainland.
　2. He is far better off now than he was three years ago.　3. He is at a loss how to solve this problem.　4. You may as well keep early hours.
　5. 你應該立個榜樣讓後人效法。　6. 他摒棄舒適和快樂而努力工作。　7. 那時候，件件事都令我驚慌失措，現在仍是如此。　8. 你喜歡怎麼稱呼它，就怎麼稱呼它。

Test 69

1. 不論天氣如何，我們都要去野餐。

___

2. 無論是晴天或下雨，天天都可以看到他。

___

3. 該型車輛是特別為嚴寒酷熱氣候所設計的。

___

4. 英語是一種重要的語言，所以很多人都在學習。

___

5. Gravity has nothing to do with the spaceships in outer space.

___

6. Let's eat something different for a change.

___

7. Your work leaves nothing to be desired.

___

8. Allowing for the flight being late, she should be back by noon.

___

【解答】

1. Whatever the weather may be, we will go for a picnic.　2. Rain or shine, he can be seen every day.　3. That type of vehicle is specially designed for severe weather conditions.　4. English is an important language, so many people are learning it.　5. 地心引力與外太空的太空船無關。 6. 我們吃點別的東西換換口味吧。　7. 你的工作十分完美。　8. 連班機誤點的時間都算在內，她也該在中午前回來。

Test 70

1. 他認識我們附近的每一個人，而我們每一個人也都認識他。

2. 要學好英文，必須下功夫。

3. 其實，只要方法正確，英文的閱讀能力並不難培養。

4. 他今天又像平常那樣，在課堂中睡著了。

5. He is so stubborn (*that*) there is no way (*of*) talking to him.

6. The indignant farmer tried to kill the villain to revenge his neighbor.

7. We believe in liberty for all.

8. Hotels around the beach area are booked to capacity in the summer.

【解答】

1. He knows everyone in our vicinity and everyone of us also knows him.
2. If you want to learn English well, you have to take pains. 3. In reality, as long as their methods are correct, their ability in reading English is not difficult to cultivate. 4. He fell asleep again in class today, as is often the case. 5. 他那麼頑固，以至於沒有辦法和他說話。
6. 這憤慨的農夫試圖殺死那個壞人，替鄰居報仇。 7. 我們相信人人都享有自由。
8. 海灘地區附近的旅館，在夏天時都被預定一空。

Test 71

1. 台灣有世界其他各地沒有的珍禽異獸。

2. 一般人都認爲長頭髮的男孩比較懶。

3. 他的誠實大部分得自父親的遺傳。

4. 這二人頑抗學校。

5. You must not forget that you may offend others unawares by what you say or do.

6. Mrs. Wang was delivered of twins last night.

7. He lost his seat on the city council.

8. Dr. Lin Yu-Tang was a paragon of the Chinese scholar.

【解答】

1. In Taiwan there are rare animals and birds that can't be found in any other place in the world. 2. Boys who wear their hair long are taken to be lazy. 3. His honesty was largely a heritage from his father. 4. The two men stood out against the school. 5. 你不可忘記你的言行可能在不知不覺中得罪別人。 6. 昨晚王太太生了（一對）雙胞胎。 7. 他未能連任市議員。 8. 林語堂博士是中國學者的典型。

Test 72

1. 她本來希望最早到的，結果反而到最晚。

_____

2. 要不要來個冰淇淋？

_____

3. 我討厭他瞪著我看的樣子。

_____

4. 中國人崇尚勤勉、節儉與純樸的生活。

_____

5. We cannot overestimate the value of computers.

_____

6. What was John wanted for?

_____

7. No food has passed my lips since yesterday.

_____

8. Most high school students are weighed down with exams.

_____

【解答】

1. Originally she had expected to be the first to arrive, but she turned out to be the last. 　2. Would you care for some ice cream? 　3. I hate the way he stares at me. 　4. The Chinese emphasize industry, frugality and living the simple life. 　5. 我們無論怎麼重視電腦都不過份。 　6. 約翰為何被通緝？ 　7. 我從昨天開始，就一直沒吃東西。 　8. 大部分高中生都被考試壓得喘不過氣來。

Test 73

1. 說我們從沒給他機會是不公平的。

_____

2. 如果有掛號信要送給我們，他就會在門口按一下鈴。

_____

3. 我衝到門口，却發現門鎖著的。

_____

4. 盡可能不要負債。

_____

5. If he had never done much good in the world, he had never done much harm.

_____

6. Courage consists not in blindly overlooking danger, but in seeing and conquering it.

_____

7. Fear aged her overnight.

_____

8. Love is like the moon, when it does not increase, it decreases.

_____

【解答】

1. It is not fair to say that we have never given him a chance.　2. If there are any registered letters for us, he will ring the doorbell.　3. I rushed to the door, only to discover that it was locked.　4. Do everything within your power not to run into debts.　5. 他在世上固然沒做過太多善事，但他也沒做過什麼惡事。　6. 勇不在於盲目的不顧危險，而在於面對危險而加以克服。　7. 恐懼使她一夜之間變老了。　8. 愛情如月亮，不增則減。

Test　74

1. 小男孩驚恐地逃離兩頭蛇。

2. 有時候我在上學的途中遇到他,他就以微笑跟我打招呼。

3. 一到需要游泳的時候,他是不輸任何人的。

4. 在老師還沒有講解課文之前,一定要自己先讀兩三遍。

5. As is often the case with sailors, he was a little too fond of liquors.

6. We find her a good daily help.

7. When it comes to singing, Mary is second to none.

8. She said she was none too early for the train.

【解答】

1. The little boy ran away from the two-headed snake in terror. 2. Sometimes I meet him on my way to school, and he greets me with a smile. 3. When it comes to swimming, he is second to none. 4. Before the teacher lectures on a lesson, they must read it two or three times in advance. 5. 他有點過份愛好杯中物,正是水手們常有的。 6. 我們發現她是個日常的好助手。 7. 如果要說唱歌,瑪麗不亞於任何人。 8. 她說她正好趕上那班火車。

Test 75

1. 我們既沒有咖啡，就用茶代替它。

_____

2. 報上說什麼地方發生了大地震？

_____

3. 她的中文作文完美無缺。

_____

4. 從小養成良好衛生習慣就不會生病。

_____

5. His arguments left me cold.

_____

6. A mother is always on the go with housekeeping.

_____

7. The accused held back the names of his partners.

_____

8. Between care and fatigue, she fell ill.

_____

【解答】

1. Since we have no coffee, we substitute tea for it.　　2. Where does the newspaper say a violent earthquake happened?　　3. Her Chinese composition leaves nothing to be desired.　　4. If we habitually pay attention to hygiene in our childhood, we won't get sick.　　5. 他的論點並沒有說動我。 6. 做母親的人，總是忙著家務。　　7. 被告不肯說出同謀者的名字。　　8. 憂慮疲乏交加，使得她病倒了。

Test 76

1. 很多學生都不太注意讀書的方法，以致於浪費許多寶貴的時間。

_____

2. 會背課本上的對話，並不表示會說英語。

_____

3. 不要讀太難的文章，也不要遇到生字就立刻查字典。

_____

4. 但是只要經常練習，任何困難都可以克服。

_____

5. The chair is a simple object of construction.

6. Many students make little of studying through the night.

_____

7. A good teacher should treat her students with firm warmness.

_____

8. Unless (you are) otherwise instructed, you are to proceed directly to Taipei.

_____

_____

【解答】

1. Many students pay so little attention to their study methods that they waste much of their precious time.　2. Being able to learn the dialogues in the textbooks by heart does not mean being able to speak English.　3. They should neither read too difficult an article, nor consult a dictionary as soon as they run into new words.　4. But as long as they practice it constantly, they will be able to overcome any difficulty.　5. 椅子是結構簡單的物體。　6. 很多學生不重視開夜車。
7. 好老師應該對學生嚴格而不失親切。　8. 若無其他指示，你可直接上台北。

Test 77

1. 我十年前小學畢業以來就沒有再見到她。

2. 許多中國學生認爲學習說英語很難。

3. 他們讀英文讀了好幾年，還是看不懂相當容易的文章。

4. 最重要的是，要能用英語說自己想說的話。

5. The fire accident was a lesson to her to be careful with gas.

6. He left his friends completely in the dark about his marriage.

7. But for the loud cry from the crowd, the carriage probably would not have stopped.

8. I have been ill with influenza for many days.

【解答】

1. I have never seen her since I graduated from elementary school ten years ago.　　2. Many Chinese students think that it is rather difficult for them to learn to speak English.　　3. They have been studying English for many years, but they still cannot understand rather easy articles.　　4. Above all, they should be able to express themselves in English.　　5. 這次火災給她一個教訓，要小心瓦斯。　　6. 他的朋友完全不知道他的婚事。　　7. 如果不是人群大聲喊叫，馬車可能不會停下來。　　8. 我得流行性感冒，已經好幾天了。

索 引

◆ 數字代表句子的號碼。符號 * 表示在註釋中。

C

J・K

L

U・V

W

翻譯句型 800

800 Translation Patterns
For Senior High School Students

售價：180 元

修　　編 / 謝　靜　芳		
發　行　所 / 學習出版有限公司	☎ (02) 2704-5525
郵 撥 帳 號 / 05127272 學習出版社帳戶	
登　記　證 / 局版台業 2179 號	
印　刷　所 / 裕強彩色印刷有限公司	
台 北 門 市 / 台北市許昌街 10 號 2F	☎ (02) 2331-4060
台灣總經銷 / 紅螞蟻圖書有限公司	☎ (02) 2795-3656
本公司網址 / www.learnbook.com.tw	
電 子 郵 件 / learnbook@learnbook.com.tw	

2019 年 10 月 1 日新修訂

ISBN 957-519-772-0

高三同學要如何準備「升大學考試」

考前該如何準備「學測」呢？「劉毅英文」的同學很簡單，只要熟讀每次的模考試題就行了。每一份試題都在7000字範圍內，就不必再背7000字了，從後面往前複習，越後面越重要，一定要把最後10份試題唸得滾瓜爛熟。根據以往的經驗，詞彙題絕對不會超出7000字範圍。每年題型變化不大，只要針對下面幾個大題準備即可。

準備「詞彙題」最佳資料：

背了再背，背到滾瓜爛熟，讓背單字變成樂趣。

考前不斷地做模擬試題就對了！

你做的題目愈多，分數就愈高。不要忘記，每次參加模考前，都要背單字、背自己所喜歡的作文。考壞不難過，勇往直前，必可得高分！

練習「模擬試題」，可參考「學習出版公司」最新出版的「7000字學測試題詳解」。我們試題的特色是：

①以「高中常用7000字」為範圍。②經過外籍專家多次校對，不會學錯。③每份試題都有詳細解答，對錯答案均有明確交待。

「克漏字」如何答題

　　第二大題綜合測驗（即「克漏字」），不是考句意，就是考簡單的文法。當四個選項都不相同時，就是考句意，就沒有文法的問題；當四個選項單字相同、字群排列不同時，就是考文法，此時就要注意到文法的分析，大多是考連接詞、分詞構句、時態等。「克漏字」是考生最弱的一環，你難，別人也難，只要考前利用這種答題技巧，勤加練習，就容易勝過別人。

準備「綜合測驗」（克漏字）可參考「學習出版公司」最新出版的「7000字克漏字詳解」。

本書特色：

1. 取材自大規模考試，英雄所見略同。
2. 不超出7000字範圍，不會做白工。
3. 每個句子都有文法分析。一目了然。
4. 對錯答案都有明確交待，列出生字，不用查字典。
5. 經過「劉毅英文」同學實際考過，效果極佳。

「文意選填」答題技巧

　　在做「文意選填」的時候，一定要冷靜。你要記住，一個空格一個答案，如果你不知道該選哪個才好，不妨先把詞性正確的選項挑出來，如介詞後面一定是名詞，選項裡面只有兩個名詞，再用刪去法，把不可能的選項刪掉。也要特別注意時間的掌控，已經用過的選項就劃掉，以免重複考慮，浪費時間。

準備「文意選填」，可參考「學習出版公司」最新出版的「7000字文意選填詳解」。

特色與「7000字克漏字詳解」相同，不超出7000字的範圍，有詳細解答。

「閱讀測驗」的答題祕訣

① 尋找關鍵字——整篇文章中，最重要就是第一句和最後一句，第一句稱為主題句，最後一句稱為結尾句。每段的第一句和最後一句，第二重要，是該段落的主題句和結尾句。從「主題句」和「結尾句」中，找出相同的關鍵字，就是文章的重點。因為美國人從小被訓練，寫作文要注重主題句，他們給學生一個題目後，要求主題句和結尾句都必須有關鍵字。

② 先看題目、劃線、找出答案、標題號——考試的時候，先把閱讀測驗題目瀏覽一遍，在文章中掃瞄和題幹中相同的關鍵字，把和題目相關的句子，用線畫起來，便可一目了然。通常一句話只會考一題，你畫了線以後，再標上題號，接下來，你找其他題目的答案，就會更快了。

③ 碰到難的單字不要害怕，往往在文章的其他地方，會出現同義字，因為寫文章的人不喜歡重覆，所以才會有難的單字。

④ 如果閱測內容已經知道，像時事等，你就可以直接做答了。

準備「閱讀測驗」，可參考「學習出版公司」最新出版的「7000字閱讀測驗詳解」，本書不超出7000字範圍，每個句子都有文法分析，對錯答案都有明確交待，單字註明級數，不需要再查字典。

「中翻英」如何準備

可參考劉毅老師的「英文翻譯句型講座實況DVD」，以及「文法句型180」和「翻譯句型800」。考前不停地練習中翻英，翻完之後，要給外籍老師改。翻譯題做得越多，越熟練。

「英文作文」怎樣寫才能得高分？

① 字體要寫整齊，最好是印刷體，工工整整，不要塗改。

② 文章不可離題，尤其是每段的第一句和最後一句，最好要有題目所說的關鍵字。

③ 不要全部用簡單句，句子最好要有各種變化，單句、複句、合句、形容詞片語、分詞構句等，混合使用。

④ 不要忘記多使用轉承語，像*at present*（現在），*generally speaking*（一般說來），*in other words*（換句話說），*in particular*（特別地），*all in all*（總而言之）等。

⑤ 拿到考題，最好先寫作文，很多同學考試時，作文來不及寫，吃虧很大。但是，如果看到作文題目不會寫，就先寫測驗題，這個時候，可將題目中作文可使用的單字、成語圈起來，寫作文時就有東西寫了。但千萬記住，絕對不可以抄考卷中的句子，一旦被發現，就會以零分計算。

⑥ 試卷有規定標題，就要寫標題。記住，每段一開始，要內縮5或7個字母。

⑦ 可多引用諺語或名言，並注意標點符號的使用。文章中有各種標點符號，會使文章變得更美。

⑧ 整體的美觀也很重要，段落的最後一行字數不能太少，也不能太多。段落的字數要平均分配，不能第一段只有一、兩句，第二段一大堆。第一段可以比第二段少一點。

準備「英文作文」，可參考「學習出版公司」出版的：